SPLASH

J.R. Hart

A NineStar Press Publication

www.ninestarpress.com

Splash

Printed in the USA

Print ISBN: 978-1-64890-084-6

First Edition, September, 2020

Also available in eBook, ISBN: 978-1-64890-083-9

WARNING:
This book contains sexually explicit content, which may only be suitable for mature readers, death of a parent, and brief references to death of a child.

Chapter One

I overslept. One week into summer, and I'd already overslept. Showering? Not really an option. Nothing about the summer after my sophomore year of college had gone the way I planned for it to go, so oversleeping? Yeah, not super unsurprising. That was me, Connor Molina, epic fuck-up. I knew why I was stuck in that godforsaken town the entire fucking summer, and almost all of it had everything to do with going to parties more often than going to my 8:00 a.m. classes. Can anyone blame that on me, though? No. The blame goes to anyone who thought morning classes would ever be an acceptable thing for anyone to experience. Whoever came up with that idea should be locked away, key thrown away, all of it.

But summer started all wrong. My ultimate goal had been to go back home. You know, normal summer stuff. Swim laps in the backyard pool, slack off, maybe hook up a few times. I don't know. Obviously, that didn't happen. I wouldn't be saying shit about that summer if it had. Uneventful stories never make for good reflections, do they? But that summer was eventful in ways I didn't expect it to be. It's part of what made my summer so, so fucked.

Instead of being home for the summer, I was there, at the Springdale Aquatic Center and Lap Pool, sitting in ungodly heat and staring at unnaturally blue-looking water. You know the kind of blue of skies and oceans and all that? No, this was hyperchlorinated blue, made more intense by the paint at the bottom until it was an intense cerulean. Instead of swimming in my parents' greenish lap pool, I was trying to make sure no one drowned in *this* lap pool. Real upgrade there, Connor. Awesome.

You'd think that shit wouldn't get old after a day and a half, but it did. The only perk was not getting audited in the first couple of days—if no one was checking to see whether I was watching closely enough, then I couldn't get screwed over and lose my job if I missed the sign. Of course, it would have been no surprise if the summer went like that. Considering everything else that had happened so far, it would have made sense for it to blow up in my stupid face and leave me jobless too. But that didn't happen. All I wanted was to make it through the summer without someone dying on my watch. That shouldn't have been too much to ask.

Nothing about the job was worth the money. If you're thinking about being a lifeguard, let this be your warning. It isn't worth it. But I couldn't back out no matter how badly I wanted to. It was on the schedule before we even had the most terrifying meeting ever, and I had no choice but to press on. Never mind that they made it clear the job was life-or-death during that meeting. Never mind that I hated the concept of ever setting foot in the pool again after the stuff their words stirred up in my mind.

Never mind that I was scared to death someone might drown right in front of me because of my own fuck-up or inability to keep them alive. Never mind the added pressure when I was already at my breaking point going into summer. All of it was horrifying, but I didn't have the luxury of choice. Everything else was full. Literally every single damn summer job...full.

If I wouldn't have had to be there in the first place, I could have slacked off and loafed around on my parents' couch and watched shitty daytime talk shows, checked out *The Price Is Right* and tried to guess the price of a car I'd never own. But no, I had rent to pay. I still do. I had to have something to do. Every pizza delivery position, every law firm secretary job, every retail cashier option, all of it was full. I couldn't even get a job sacking groceries, not that I would have taken a position clearly made for a high schooler. Any of those had to be better than lifeguarding though. Every job in town, even that, was for teenagers. I was underqualified for the good shit, but I was way overqualified for being a lifeguard.

One summer. I promised them I'd work there for one summer, but after that, I had told myself there was no way in hell I'd ever be caught on that guard stand again. The whole job is complete and utter bullshit. No amount of SPF in the world could have gotten me through it either. I still don't know how I didn't lose my entire mind being there. Well, I do, but I didn't at the time.

Sure, I probably took it a little bit too seriously, a little bit too personally whenever they mentioned, you know...drowning. None of my other coworkers gave a shit if someone were to die in their section. The thing is, they're all basically kids, lifeguards are. High school babies at best, with a few going into college in the fall. I was the only jackass actually *in* college when I got the job, so, of course, none of them took it seriously. It made sense that they didn't give a shit if something happened. None of us ever think it'll happen to us. No one ever does, do they? But that stuff *does* happen. It does. I had seen it happen before, and the thought of letting it happen that summer somehow? I was horrified by the entire prospect.

Don't worry, nobody actually drowned over the summer, though the close calls were enough to make me hate the job regardless.

The summer didn't start great, either. We were down two guards on the second day of work. One of them never bothered to call in, and I'm pretty sure she never showed up all summer anyway. The other one missed the audit ball and got sent home. Greg, the manager, tossed this little ball in the water in your section. Each ball represents someone drowning, and if you don't jump in and save the ball in time, you get written up and sent home early. I'm not sure why they think sending you home is the right choice there. It's not like it gives you more practice. To me, you should be buddy-guarding until you get it right, but that's not how it goes, and it left us shorthanded. *Way* too shorthanded.

That's why I scan the water, why I always keep scanning the water. The ball represents a life, someone she would have just let drown because she wasn't even watching. Getting sent home was the least of her worries. Maybe if it had been a real person, she would have understood. We hadn't been working together long enough for me to even know her name, and by the third audit she missed in two weeks, she was fired, so I never really got to know her anyway.

I don't switch off when I'm working. I can't. You never know who the hell might end up drowning on your watch, and I wasn't about to have a death on my conscience. I couldn't fathom the idea of telling someone's mom, "hey, your kid drowned because I wasn't paying attention," or somehow having to deal with the consequences there, the nightmares or whatever else. It's stuff like that making the job literally the worst in the world. If I looked away, who knows what might have happened? Maybe someone would have died. I don't know. Maybe I was just fucking paranoid. Maybe I still am.

Or maybe it's the way my section always attracted the biggest jackasses on the planet. The entire time I was working the first few days, regardless of the section I was in, there was this one guy. One damn kid who had to show off, basically. He and his buddies were there to break every rule, doing flips off the high dive, trying to play chicken. They were old enough to know better and old enough also to set a bad example for anyone younger—if they could do it, the younger kids thought it was safe to do too. It was impossible to watch everyone in my section when he kept pulling my focus, making me watch him and his friends carefully so nobody got killed.

He was there when I was manning the diving boards, attempting cannonballs and flips far beyond his skill level. When I moved on to the wide slide typically reserved for kids to slide down with his parents, he and his friends were shoving each other down and trying to launch themselves off. I'd tell him to sit on his ass (in nicer words) and not on his stomach, but halfway down he'd spin, flipping to skid down headfirst.

"He's cute, isn't he?" I can still remember James asking me that question and even now, a huge part of me wants to slap him over it.

"The one with the death wish? No, he's not." I didn't get it. I didn't understand how half of the guards at this pool could think he was hot. I was there trying to watch, trying to keep track of everyone, and it felt like everyone else was simply there to gawk at the patrons. Being the only one actually there to work sucked, even if I got that they were just kids. You know, whatever, but some of us didn't need the added distraction.

"You have to admit he's at least a little bit cute," James said, elbowing me in the ribs. I was half tempted to break his arm over the way he jabbed me.

"I don't have to. He's not being cute. He's trying to crack his head open on the side of the pool. What are you doing over here anyway?" This wasn't James's section right then, not where I was, and I couldn't understand why he was even where I was at, to be honest. Last I saw, he was supposed to be over by the lazy river, not close to me in the deep end.

"I'm on break," he told me.

"Oh, so you're over here lurking and trying to stare at him and everything else, getting in my way when I'm trying to do my job? Cool. Thanks." I was only half joking. I tried to make myself seem as pleasant as possible, but a large part of me was really annoyed. The last thing I needed was James near me, trying to talk while I was taking this seriously. James was the only other openly gay guard there, and not even a small part of me was surprised he was interested in a dumbass like that one. I never tried to hide who I was, and if a girl at the pool flirted with me, she usually figured out she wasn't my type pretty quickly. But James? He couldn't hide it. Anyone could've clocked him from a mile away. He wasn't subtle and it was okay, but it also got him in trouble. The town wasn't the most open-minded place ever.

I was over it. Over the job, over James's obsession with the worst patrons, over the high school garbage. None of that was James's fault, of course. He didn't know any better. He was just a kid, fresh out of high school, a baby gay coming into his own. Of *course,* he thought every guy thrust in front of him was hot as hell. He was young, horny, attracted to stupidity. I couldn't blame him for wanting to know more about this jock who couldn't stay out of my section. But really? This particular guy? I couldn't help but think James had no taste at all.

The guy was a problem. I could have sworn the first few days he was watching me, waiting for me to turn around to watch someone else, so he could do another stupid thing like I wasn't going to see it coming. You know how every mom in America says she's got eyes in the back of her head? Over that summer, I completely understood the sentiment. When someone's up to no good literally all the time, you don't have to look directly at them to know they're in trouble. And that guy, he was *always* in trouble. I'd turn away for a second, turn back, and he'd have someone smaller crawling up on his shoulders or be tossing someone around and into the water. For me, it became obvious he was trying to get hurt, to get all eyes on him. Blowing my whistle didn't help.

Another time, I skipped the whistle altogether, knowing he wouldn't pay attention. "Get down," I shouted toward him. I knew he could hear me. Stepping closer to the edge of the pool close to the in-pool rock wall made it more obvious I was talking to him specifically, because I was practically within slapping distance of him as he tried to hang by one arm, dangling over the pool. He still chose to ignore me. "Seriously, if you keep doing that, I'm going to get the manager!" Even my most professional tone couldn't mask how pissed off I was in that moment, and worse, I knew I sounded like a kid trying to tattle.

If his hand slipped, he could fall, maybe on someone below him. Hell, maybe he'd bang his face on the rocks, skid down, make the pool a bloody mess. I didn't want to clean it up, and I know nobody else did. Besides, it would have messed up the face everyone thought was so cute.

"Ooh, I'll have to get the manager," he said, changing his pitch and waggling his head to mock me. He had the nerve to talk back to me like he knew how much it would bug me. "Hey, pretty boy, can't you let it slide for once? We're just trying to have a good time is all."

"And what happens, *pretty boy,* when you smack someone's head on the side of the pool, and you start to drown, and I have to save y'all's sorry asses?" I spit the words back at him. I knew it was unprofessional, but I didn't care. I couldn't stay professional when he was pushing every single one of my buttons in the worst way. "If you can't follow the rules, leave. Or I'll *make* you leave."

"Ooooh." His little chorus of cronies had quite the reply to that. I could've sworn I was going to lose my shit on the entire crew. But him dropping off the wall and swimming over closer to me, less than slapping distance and right into my personal bubble, only threw me off. He got closer like he knew I wasn't going to make good on my threats and it made me even more frustrated. I desperately wanted to kick him. Obviously, I couldn't, but I wanted to. He had some kind of nerve.

"Looks like pretty boy here thinks he's hot shit since he has this little whistle around his neck," he said, looping his finger through my lanyard. He tugged me a little closer, and I jerked backward. "Don't worry, I won't pull you in. I'm just trying to get a better look at—"

"Well, don't," I said. I stared him down with fury and frustration. I couldn't imagine someone being so rude, so petulant, not at that age. It wasn't like he was a child, but he was sure as hell acting like one. I swore to myself if there was one more problem, I'd make sure he was banned from the pool for the rest of the season. But then it was time to rotate sections. My next one was the kiddie section. This was good news. For fifteen minutes, he wouldn't be my problem. Sure, little kids could easily drown in like, six inches of water, but at least they attempted to follow the rules most of the time. They weren't wild like this guy and his friends. For those few moments, he wasn't my responsibility and I felt relief. Even if he drowned from his stupid antics at that point, he wasn't my problem anymore.

I tried to steal a sympathetic glance at Maria—she was easily my favorite lifeguard—since she'd taken over where I had been, but I realized quickly the guy wasn't there anymore. It was hard not to feel annoyed or personally attacked. I was getting the impression that as soon as I left an area, he did too. I tried to convince myself it was more likely he'd gone home or went to the snack shack or something, but mostly I felt a little victimized, like he was trying to target my section to make me deal with his bullshit. None of that mattered, though, because I got to have lifeguard swim after the kiddie pool time.

Lifeguard swim was my one moment of relief. I didn't have to watch anyone during that time. I knew I should be swimming laps during my free time, keeping myself in shape for the fall, for the swim team, but after dealing with *him,* all I wanted to do was cool off and relax. That's why I made a beeline for the lazy river and grabbed a tube someone had abandoned. I hopped in, leaned back, and closed my eyes to take a break, shifting until I was comfortable. Patrons can't get in the pool during lifeguard swim, obviously, because if the lifeguards are swimming, they can't watch them. It made sense that I'd be able to relax during that time, right? Except no. As soon as I got relaxed, reclining in the inner tube, getting a little tan or whatever, I started getting splashed.

It came with the territory since little kids would dip their toes in the water while waiting to get back in the pool. I understood. It was hard being five years old or something and being told you couldn't swim for fifteen minutes, but when I opened my eyes and took a peek at the culprit, I was frustrated. Scratch that, I was downright pissed off. No, of *course,* it wasn't a kid. It was the same stupid guy, splashing me for no apparent reason. "What the hell?" I know I should have asked questions with a more professional attitude, should have toned down my language, but I'm telling you, he was already well past getting under my skin. "I'm trying to take a break." I could've sworn he'd never had a job before in his life. If he had, there was no way he'd want to ruin my day, mess up the few okay moments I had by splashing the fuck out of me.

He didn't answer me; instead, he laughed and turned to his friends, getting a high five from one of them as I floated out of his reach. *Classy.* I figured he was done, and I closed my eyes, letting myself drift, but within minutes, *bam.* This time, it wasn't a splash. He soaked me with a complete dousing of water. It was clear he was following me; my inner tube hadn't made it all the way around the pool yet. It was a few feet from where he'd been as if he was deliberately walking along the side to get me.

That was enough. Instead of playing it cool, I found myself jumping out of the tube, struggling against the current in the moving water to stalk over and give him a piece of my mind. "Listen up, buddy. I'm real freakin' sick of you and whatever kind of bullshit you're trying to pull here. I can't even take a break without you getting in my way. I don't know what your problem is, but could you maybe not be a jackass for like, five minutes or something?" I was hissing the words, and I wanted to punch him. I understand it's not appropriate to talk to someone who was paying to be in that establishment. I know it was shitty, okay? But he was being way shittier to me, and I couldn't take it anymore without losing my cool. I'm seriously lucky he didn't report me and get my ass fired right then. He could have.

"Hey, man, be chill. It was an accident." He swung his feet in the water, brushing my leg with his toes and giving a slight grin. I tried to swat his foot away, but he did it again, grazing my skin with the tip of his foot. "I wasn't trying to get you wet. I promise." For half a second, he almost seemed sincere. "You have a little something—" he leaned forward and wiped at my cheek with his fingers. "—right there."

"Thanks," I huffed back. I was being sarcastic, but he didn't seem to notice, flashing me a broader smile instead. I'm telling you, his life goal was to drive me insane over the summer, and I was positive of it at that point. If one of us didn't make it out alive, well, I wouldn't have been surprised. He seemed destined to make my own personal hell a few circles deeper, torturing me on a daily basis.

Chapter Two

I honestly hoped telling him off after he splashed me would be the end of it, that I'd be done with him if he got the hint. But he didn't, making his way to my section after the pool opened the next day.

"Hey," he said, walking past me. "It's my favorite lifeguard." He winked at me, like flirting was in any way okay after how he'd acted the day before. I wanted to scream, but rolling my eyes was just about the only thing I could do without risking losing my job, so that's what I did. Then, I turned my entire body toward the other part of my section. It should have given him a hint, but I should have expected he'd be hard to shake. "Well fine, I didn't want to talk to you anyway," he snorted at me. I swear to God, I almost strangled him.

Part of me felt if I gave him less attention, he'd only push for more, try harder to get my focus on him. I was pretty sure he was just showing off, anyway, and I decided to take the opposite approach. Maybe if I gave him a small amount of attention, he'd give up, I figured, so I turned and gave him a small wave and then focused harder on what I'd been looking at: the small cluster of kids in front of me. But then a hand wrapped around my ankle, startling me. I'm sure I jumped out of my skin.

"What the hell?" I jerked my leg, trying hard to get out of his grasp, so he let go. I'll be honest, it freaked me out a little bit the way he'd grabbed me so unexpectedly. He hadn't hurt me. He'd *scared* me.

"I yelled for you, but you didn't hear me," he said. "I thought if I nudged you, maybe you'd talk to me." It wasn't a nudge. It was a full-on grab. But it also seemed innocent enough, and the way he looked up at me, eyes twinkling with all sorts of mischief, made me feel the so-called nudge was the least of my worries anyway.

"What do you need?" I asked him impatiently, glaring down at him. I didn't have time for this, and I was hoping my demeanor said as much.

"I just wanted to know what your name is, pretty boy." He grinned.

"Why? Are you planning on turning me in for yelling at you the other day or what?" I asked him. I couldn't think of a single reason he might want my name other than to continue ruining my summer. Adding me getting fired to the list of ways he'd fucked with me thus far would have made total sense. It wasn't even like I didn't almost sort of deserve it, even if it was in response to the things he was doing. I'd lost my cool and gone off on him. I deserved to be fired.

"No. I'm not turning you in, don't worry. I just wanted to know your name, pretty boy. Assuming you don't always go by 'pretty boy.'"

"I don't ever go by 'pretty boy,'" I snapped. "I'm Connor." I was sure he'd never drop it if I didn't give him a name. He was propped up on the side of the pool, elbows resting on the edge as he gazed up at me. I glanced down and then back up to keep scanning the water. I can't even explain how he looked at me, but even when I wasn't paying attention to him, his eyes were on me. I could feel them. It was unnerving.

"I like the name Connor. It suits you." He smiled, and I considered pushing him back into the water. "You look like you're about my age. How old are you, Connor?" Now, he had my name, and it seemed like he was going to take every opportunity he had to say it just to piss me off.

"Older than you." I wasn't about to stand there and let myself get interrogated by a complete idiot. There was no use telling him he was obviously, completely younger than me and we both knew it. His actions alone spoke volumes.

"Cool. I'm Tristan. Later!" As quickly as he'd shown up at my feet, he was gone, darting through the water after pushing off the wall without any other conversation, disappearing into the waves caused by everyone around him swimming and playing in the pool. I had no idea what to make of him, but everything he did left me feeling on edge. And because he had my name, I was worried he wasn't telling the truth, that he'd turn me in the second he had a chance. By late afternoon, I still hadn't been called into the office, so it started to seem like maybe he was being honest after all. Still, I wasn't ready to let my guard down. Not really.

He also wasn't acting as wild as he had been by late afternoon, which made me wonder if he got the point that I was annoyed without me having to tell him anymore. At the time, I thought if I could get through the summer without Tristan acting as dumb as he had to begin with and without anyone getting seriously hurt, then everything would be fine. I'd let the other shit slide. The thing was, Tristan couldn't let it slide, could he? He couldn't sit there and let me have a normal fucking summer. No, he had to go and screw everything up, because, of *course,* he did.

The next day, he was back in my section, this time, over near the lily pads. They were these slippery circles you could run across, trying to stay upright. He was back to screwing around like he'd been doing to begin with. It was an effort to draw every lick of attention he could get from me. The difference now was he wasn't breaking any rules, so not only could I not turn him in, I also had the out on watching him. I could take the opposite approach of what I'd done the day before. Instead of giving him the attention he was seeking, I decided not to give him any at all. As far as I could tell, he was just goofing off, and unless I could call him out on breaking the rules, I wasn't wasting my energy or getting all stressed out over him. I did what anyone else would have done: I focused on the younger kids who were holding the ropes above their head, meant to steady them. Waiting their turn, they moved across very carefully. Tristan was nice enough to wait his turn behind them, even letting a kid go ahead of him in line. When it was his turn, he bolted across, whooping and hollering the whole way. It was fine, but it was incredibly grating, getting under my skin in the worst way.

Later, I moved on to the lap pool, which was a few feet away from the aquatic part that had the slides and lazy river and kids' sections. The lap pool was deeper, wider, meant for people there to swim and not just splash and have fun. Usually, serious swimmers stayed over in this side, and they didn't get in as much trouble as the younger kids and teens did, so watching them was lower effort.

Lower effort didn't mean no effort, because even experienced swimmers could get hurt and the lap pool was open to anyone to use, even if they weren't swimming laps. I still had to keep scanning, turning my head one way and then the other. When I turned back, someone was deep under the water. I couldn't see who they were, but they were tall, and the fact that Tristan wasn't anywhere to be seen made me uneasy. Whoever this was had been down for a while, too long, longer than I thought they should have been able to hold their breath. Panic rose in me. I could hear my heart beating in my ears. Time felt frozen. I tried to count seconds in case they were barely under for a bit, but I lost all concept of numbers in that moment. I had no idea if that person had been under for a minute, two minutes, and I didn't know what to do. Every speck of training I had escaped me. I didn't know how to handle a drowning. I did, but suddenly I didn't.

And then he floated to the top, facedown. I panicked. Fuck, my brain was like that: fuck, fuck, *fuck*. I felt like I'd possibly cursed him, thinking and believing—hell, even telling him—he would drown if he didn't stop. And yeah, it was absolutely obviously Tristan, because, of course. Who else would it be? It couldn't have been any other patron in the entire damn world. It had to be him, the eternal thorn in my side.

At that point, it didn't matter. Nothing mattered, not the paperwork I'd have to do over this, not the fact I'd probably lose my job. All I could think about was the fact that in an effort not to give Tristan attention, I'd probably just caused him to die. I jumped in the water, but I was so terrified my limbs didn't seem to work. It felt like I was swimming in peanut butter, water feeling too thick to be actual water. A huge part of me worried I'd never be able to carry his long, lean, muscular body to the side of the pool. He was younger than me but taller, bigger, probably heavier. My mind raced. What if I'd forgotten how to do CPR? How could I save him?

None of that mattered, either, not as I pushed through the water, attempting long strokes with my arms to get there, wrap those arms around him, and get him turned faceup. I was holding him close to my body, an arm guiding him through the water, doing anything I could to swim with his dead weight attached to me. I heaved him up on the side of the pool. A few people crowded around to see what was happening, but that didn't matter to me either. I barely noticed them until after. I was focused on Tristan.

I started with small pumps to his chest, ineffective ones because I was way too hesitant to make a difference. My fear was taking over, my nerves and my bad memories. I reminded myself I'd have to crack his ribs on the next round if I genuinely wanted to help him. First, though, he needed air. I had to put air into his lungs the only way I knew how, and I'd figure out the rest in a minute.

I did what I had to do, tilting his head back and forgetting anyone around me. All I wanted was for him to breathe. *Come on, Tristan, breathe. Breathe, Tristan, come on.* It was a steady rhythm on repeat in my brain. I was breathing all my air into him, and for a half a second, I thought I was hallucinating, lightheaded. I thought I could feel his lips move, like I'd felt his tongue try to flutter against my teeth or something. I was certain I was a crazy person, thinking he was somehow trying to kiss me or something. Or, I thought that until I felt the tug around my neck.

My whistle. Tristan was awake and I definitely wasn't imagining it. The tongue movement, the lips, everything was real. I wanted to freak out and rip myself away from him and scream and potentially punch him because how the hell could he be so stupid? Didn't he know I thought he had died? Didn't he know drownings aren't shit anyone should mess with or fake or fuck around with?

Somehow, I was still down there, still pretending to breathe for him. For half a second, I did the very stupid thing of sort of, kind of, maybe a little bit kissing him back. It wasn't because I wanted to give in to what he wanted. It was because I wanted him to know I knew he was faking it. I let my tongue into his mouth and then I backed off and backed up and got away from what I was doing. When he propped himself up on his elbows, his eyes drooped. For a moment, I feared I'd made a mistake. Maybe he hadn't been trying to kiss me after all, and I'd just imagined it, and I was being a dumbass. If that was the case, kissing him back was the wrong direction, and he was probably going to turn me in, the ever-running fear in my brain.

But then he sat up the rest of the way, smiling and saying "my hero" as he winked at me. He fucking winked, the nerve. People were applauding me for saving him, but I felt confused and a little sick. So, I did the logical thing and I ran off and closed myself in the office. The last thing I wanted was to look at Tristan or anyone else who had seen what happened. If I did, there was a good chance I might drown him myself.

Chapter Three

Paperwork was fine. I could do the stupid paperwork. The fact I had to fill the forms out with Tristan right there pissed me off beyond belief. I had to actually talk to him, sit in the same room looking at his stupid smug face, and I was furious at him. We were alone in the manager's office, which was a bad choice given the near-hatred I felt for him. Why the fuck anyone left me alone with someone I wanted to straight-up murder at that point was beyond me, but then, no one else knew how pissed I was.

"Were you ever—for one second even—actually drowning?" I asked him right after the door closed, but I didn't really give him the chance to answer. We both knew the answer anyway. "You pulled a stupid stunt like that, scared me half to death, made me drag your heavy ass across the pool, all to, y'know, be totally fine? Screw you, man."

I was biting my tongue quite a bit even with all I said, holding back from going off on him all the way, and I had to keep my voice low. I was praying no one was listening, but when I realized I was ranting, I stopped. Tristan, for his part, didn't really respond at all. Instead, he sat there and covered his mouth with his hand like he was suppressing a smirk. "You think this is funny?"

"It's not as serious as you're makin' it out to be, pretty boy," he said, taking a step toward me, and then another, till I was backed against the door. "You take it all so seriously, don't you? Let loose a little once in a while." He looped his finger through my whistle lanyard again.

"Drowning *is* serious. Have you ever seen a person drown? Or watched what happens when they don't come up? It's fucking serious. Not that you'd know, given how you just pretended to do it like it's no big deal, but people die from shit like that all the time and you think it's cute and funny. And then on top of that you have the nerve to call me 'pretty boy'? Really? Say it again. Call me that one more time, and I swear to God I'll—" At that point, I had to cut myself off before I made any actual threats. I was on thin fucking ice already with how I'd cursed at him and all, but he deserved that much. "Let me get this paperwork done so I can get back to work. You've cut into my day enough already."

All Tristan did was chuckle at me, taking a couple of exaggerated steps backward. "As you wish. What do you need to know?"

"What's your name?" I read the first line of the form off.

"I already told you. It's Tristan."

"Tristan *what?*" As if he didn't know I needed a last name. He was such a smartass. Come *on.*

"Tristan McCarthy. You want a middle name too? Grandparents' name, color of my favorite pair of underwear, social security number, ice cream flavor?"

I rolled my eyes. "Hey, the only reason you're in here having to do this with me is because of your stupid idea to fake drown, so don't cop an attitude with me," I said. "I need your age."

"Just turned nineteen," he told me. A year younger than me, a whole hell of a lot of years stupider than me. No surprise there.

"Phone number?" I asked.

"Oh, wow, I barely kiss you and you're already wanting my number? That's so hot." I was so close to giving him a faceful of my clipboard. I could almost picture smacking him with it, but I couldn't exactly explain him walking out of the office with a bloody nose, could I?

"It's for the stupid form," I snapped, as if he didn't already know that.

"I'm just giving you hell, pret—Connor," he corrected himself last-second, as if he knew how close I was to absolutely going off on him. "Seriously, do you always look like you've got a stick up your ass? Breathe." He mimicked deep, meditative breaths.

"I was breathing. Or I was trying to get you to breathe, but I guess you were doing a fine job of that on your own, weren't you? Now. Phone number." This time, it wasn't a question. I was demanding it.

"You're mad at me?" he asked, dodging the question and dipping his head like he was trying to meet my eyes. I tried not to look at him, didn't *want* to look at him, but I couldn't help it.

"I asked for your phone number," I said, getting sick and tired of repeating myself on the same line over and over.

"Yeah, and I'll tell you. Just give me a sec. But I've been answering all of your questions, and you haven't answered a single one of mine," Tristan said.

"These are things I have to ask for my job, not some stupid shit interrogation you've got going on here," I told him. "Faking a drowning, then kissing me? Real funny. You think I'm going to tell you shit after you did that?"

"I wasn't trying to be funny," he said solemnly. "But I will give you my phone number. If you'll promise to use it sometime, of course."

"That's not how this works! It's not how any of it works. You can't pull a stunt like that and then demand I call you after. That's not the point of the form. You have to give your number to us for legal reasons, so we can make sure you're not, uh"—I looked at my form—"dry drowning or anything."

"You could come find out in person," he said. I tried to ignore his comment. I genuinely did, but he wouldn't stop pushing. "It's really too bad, actually. All of that, the ages spent on paperwork, me going to all of that trouble, heck, almost drowning to death, and you turned out to be a pretty crummy kisser."

"I wasn't kissing you!" I yelled and then lowered my voice again, almost growling the words at him. "I was trying to save your miserable ass, not kiss you. I can kiss just fine." It was the most ridiculous, most childish argument on my end, but I'll be damned if anyone ever says I'm a shitty kisser, no matter how transparent his argument was in hindsight.

"Oh, are you? Because that out there was pretty lame." He leaned against the office counter, eyeing me and biting his lip. Jesus, I don't think I'd ever been madder in my life. "I wasn't impressed," he told me.

"You're such an asshole." I stepped closer to him to make my point clearer. "You put me through living hell. You pretended to drown. You could have died from pretending, you know that, right? You could have actually died, kicked the damn bucket trying to do that. You almost cost me my job, because now it looks like I wasn't watching the water closely enough because you've been such a...a...a...nightmare! And now you want to say I'm a bad kisser on top of all of that? It wasn't even a kiss!" In my anger, I'd gotten nose to nose with him almost. "CPR isn't a fucking joke. You're being a real douchebag if you think it's okay to call something that serious a kiss. That's not even remotely a kiss at all," I said again. "This is."

I grabbed his arms hard, pulling him closer and pressing my lips to his. I'm not sure why I did it outside of proving a point, and when I did, I was giving it my all, releasing every ounce of frustration at everything he'd done so far that summer all into one kiss. It was stupid but it felt important and overwhelming, necessary to put him in his place.

But he kissed back, slipping his tongue into my mouth, and I found myself grasping at his lower back, at the bare skin his swimming trunks didn't cover. When he cupped a hand around my head, I melted into it, but when he weaved his other hand between us, tugged at my lanyard, I remembered why this was happening in the first place. I was proving a point, and he was messing it all up. I stepped back and tried to regain my composure.

"I said I needed your phone number." The last thing I wanted was to acknowledge what I'd just done, so I didn't. I couldn't have been more unprofessional than that, and saying anything about it just made things worse. I wanted to pretend it had never happened in the first place.

"Are you going to use it if I give it to you? I mean, I'd like you to. I didn't give you nearly enough credit, Connor," he said. He was so fucking smug. Most of me wanted to slap him, but a tiny part of me was proud I'd changed his mind. I was sick.

"Just give me the number," I told him. There was no way in hell I planned to ever use it.

Chapter Four

Two days off for dealing with emotional trauma wasn't nearly enough. They gave it to me, because apparently when you save a life, they figure you need healing time. I hadn't saved anybody, not really. They didn't know that. But I definitely *did* need the healing time, if only to keep from strangling Tristan the next time I saw him. Unfortunately for me and my healing time, James decided the first break of my first day back to work was the right time to bring all of what happened back to the forefront of my brain.

"What was it like?" he asked me. I already knew what he was talking about. How could I not know? It was all anyone was talking about, obviously. I'd already had several coworkers ask me what it was like seeing Tristan almost die, what giving CPR to a real person instead of a dummy felt like. They had all kinds of questions about the drowning. If nothing else, Tristan's fake crisis woke them up a little bit to the reality that it could happen, and for that I *was* thankful, even if I hated him a little bit.

"What was what like?" I had to play dumb. I didn't want to indulge his questions, not when I was trying to get my mind off it entirely.

"What was it like basically, you know...kissing him?" James asked me. Leave it to him to be an epic dumbass. I already knew the kind of guy he was. Young, and a little worried he wouldn't get enough action in the godforsaken town we lived in. With the town being near a college, it was progressive enough to get by, but everywhere else near us was backward as fuck, and I got where he was coming from. It didn't matter where he was coming from though. Equating a life-or-death situation to a kiss was almost as annoying as when Tristan had done the same. At least James wasn't trying to get anything from me out of it.

"I didn't kiss him," I said. As far as anyone knew, it was strictly professional CPR, and I fully intended on keeping it that way. No one knew the reality of the situation, and no one knew what happened in the office when Tristan and I were alone. No one needed to. "I tried to save his life. There's a difference, James." The condescension was obvious in my tone, but James seemed unfazed.

"I meant basically, not really," he said. "You had your lips on his lips though. Were they soft? I bet they were so soft." His eyes fluttered like he was daydreaming what it would be like to kiss Tristan, whether it was CPR or not.

"Are you seriously, genuinely asking me if his lips were soft? What part of 'I literally thought he was dying' didn't connect with you? Do you actually think I gave a single fuck about his lips and not the fact he wasn't breathing?" His lips *were* soft, but that wasn't the point in the slightest. If the summer got any longer, I was going to end up with what amounted to a hit list of stupid people. Tristan would have been the first name on it, and James felt like a good close second.

All the bullshit was too much for me. Some of it probably stemmed from me desperately needing to get laid. I swear to God, Tristan may have thought I was moody because I had some sort of stick up my ass, but the reality was I hadn't had a moment to have anything up my ass—stick or otherwise—in a decent amount of time. That wasn't helping me at all, and I had somehow, over the course of two days, chalked up my ill-advised kiss in the office to general grumpiness over my lack of action. But the same mood it put me in wasn't helping me try to avoid strangling the people who pissed me off, and James was being stupid. Him being an idiot combined with my shitty mood left me agitated well beyond my usual limit.

"I just...I don't know. I figured you could tell me," he said, dejected. "Besides, Jess said she thought she saw some tongue action happen when you were down there."

"Tongue action? Are you fucking kidding me? It was CPR! There wasn't any tongue action." Obviously, there was what James was calling tongue action, but no one needed to know about it. If it wouldn't have made matters worse, I would have told off Jess too. That bitch! "He. Was. Dying. I saved his life. Can you stop grilling me for like, five seconds please?" I snapped at him. It wasn't James's fault, not really, but I couldn't do this right then.

"Fine," he said. It was obvious I'd upset him. "I'm not trying to, I don't know. Whatever. He's just hot and the only way I'm ever going to find out if he has nice lips is by living vicariously through you, so I guess I'll have to live with not knowing how great he is for the rest of my damn life." He was being really over-the-top mopey about the whole thing and for a second, I halfway felt sorry for him until I remembered this was Tristan we were talking about.

"He isn't hot," I said.

"Come on, you can't even admit it? Even if you don't like him, he's objectively at least a little bit hot. You can think someone is annoying and still think they're hot," James pushed. I wanted to kick him. Hard.

Sure, okay, I could see where he was coming from. A lot about Tristan was hot. Hair that wasn't quite blond or brown, a small crooked smile, perfect teeth that showed every time he bit his lip. Long, lean body that made evident the amount of work he probably put into it, either here or in the gym. Ugh. I hated James for making me even think about it. Tristan was maybe, a little bit, a tiny sort of piece in the back of my mind, possibly, kind of attractive to me. But the attitude and his personality wiped all of that away. James was still rambling about him, and I snapped back to focus.

"God, what I wouldn't give to play chicken with him just once...prop myself up on those sexy shoulders. He looks so good like that. He could grab my legs...ungghhh... I need to start coming up here on my days off, I think."

I rolled my eyes. Poor, naïve James. "You realize playing chicken is against the rules, right? And hitting on patrons? And—"

"I know the rules. Goddamn, do you ever have any fun?"

I didn't know why everyone felt the need to call me out on not having enough fun. This wasn't supposed to be fun. Nothing about the summer was going to be fun, and I was sure of it. At that point in the summer, all I'd done was get up, go to class, go to the pool to work, and then go back to my apartment to study and have zero fun whatsoever. What part of summer meant fun when you were twenty? None of it. "Fine, whatever. You know what? You're right. Go for it. Get his number. Best of luck to you," I said. I didn't want to crush his dreams just because I was more jaded than he was. It was easy to forget he was eighteen and basically still a kid.

"He's probably straight anyway," James lamented, but I could tell he was mulling it over for a second. "You really think I should try?"

"I think you'd be an idiot to try, honestly, because he seems like a terrible person to me, straight or not straight. But you know, do whatever you want. I won't be the moral compass cricket following you and telling you not to do it if it's what you really want." I was tired of trying to police what anyone did at that point. Their relationships were their problems, and if they didn't involve me in it, even better. If James wanted to date someone who thought fake-drowning to kiss a guy was cool, more power to him, but the thought he was doing it made me feel sorry for him. Really? That was his idea of a good summer? Hooking up with Tristan?

James had basically wasted my entire break with his stupid line of questioning too. I was trying to eat my hot dog, get back to work, and instead he'd made me nauseated solely by bringing up the stupid not-kiss, which only made me think of the actual kiss I was dumb enough to fall into Tristan's trap for. It didn't matter. I had zero time to think about this today, so I half-shoved the hot dog down my throat and got back to work. I couldn't escape from how much I didn't want to think about how shitty my summer was as a whole by that point.

When I tried to focus on work, all I could see was James hovering over Tristan, standing near him and trying to be flirty. James was already five minutes late coming back from break. Tristan kept looking over at me, and it sort of felt like he was thinking it was somehow *my* fault James was over there. I could tell that's what he was doing by his small glare. You know what? I didn't give a fuck. It was all annoying, but none of it was my issue. In a way, I was almost cheering for James to succeed, not because I wanted to inevitably have to hear him recount every single detail of their sex lives, and certainly not because I wanted to listen to him mope over the eventual crash and burn, but because all of that would have been far better than Tristan constantly being in my section and in my life. Besides, James deserved something good. He sucked, but he sucked less than some of the other guards.

But after James finally got yelled at to get back to work, he slunk past me on his way to his section, looking pretty damn defeated. We were close enough to each other's sections that we could talk, so I let him, as much as I didn't care.

"How'd it go?" It was pretty obvious by how he acted, but I was feigning innocence anyway, in the name of not being a shitty...friend? Coworker? Whatever?

"I got shot down, I guess," he admitted. The 'I guess' made it seem like he wasn't entirely willing to accept what happened, or that he thought he could change it, but the rest of his attitude made it pretty clear: it was a complete, total shutdown.

"He tell you why?" I asked him. "Straight after all, or what?" That was the part I was genuinely interested in: why Tristan would shut him down. He clearly wanted to hook up with someone this summer, and it was weird he hadn't leaped at the opportunity. James wasn't entirely unfortunate looking. He was your average, everyday skinny-ass twink without any real meat on his bones, but he was cute enough, putting in effort on his hair, even if his pomade was going to get washed out during a lifeguard swim or something. His problem was, when it came to talking to guys, he was hella desperate and ridiculously needy. Thankfully, he knew better than to try anything with me.

"He said I'm cute," James started with, which sounded hopeful more than anything. "Then he said he hopes I have a good summer, but he's kind of already got his eye on somebody else. He doesn't want to get my hopes up in case he gets a shot with the person he's really after. I don't know, maybe he is straight. He was really vague, you know?"

"That...that really sucks," I said. Dammit, I wanted to avoid looking at him, but when I did see him, it was obvious he was staring at me as I talked to James. I was torn: get involved, try to give James a shot with him by telling Tristan there wasn't a chance in hell I was interested in him at all, or give Tristan the cold shoulder until he hopefully eventually figured it out himself. Or, I guess it was possible I could do nothing, give zero shits, and hope that both of them moved on to other, better people. No one really deserved a shot at someone like Tristan, I thought, someone who would fake a drowning for attention or whatever else. If that was his go-to move, who knew what sort of harm I'd be putting James in by trying to get them together. The poor kid would not know what hit him, and that hardly seemed fair. It was a train crash waiting to happen and pushing them together would be like flipping the switch for a collision course.

I wasn't sure how the hell I managed to get involved in so much drama during a stupid summer job. It wasn't like I asked for any of it. I was just trying to make a little money, but somehow that's how life is for me: Shit goes down, and I get sucked into it whether I want to or not. *Fuck*. I was absolutely certain this was going to be the longest, worst, most miserable summer ever at that point.

Chapter Five

"Hey." Tristan. Of course. The trash bags in my hands weren't going to take themselves out, and he wasn't about to make it worse by boring me to death with whatever he had to say. I did the only thing I could do in that situation: I acted like I didn't hear him speaking at all.

"Connor! Hey," he said again. Unfortunately, he didn't give up easily, and the fact he was using his knowledge of my name against me wasn't helping. When he stepped in front of me and tried to catch my eye, I couldn't keep pretending like I didn't hear him anymore, and that was annoying as hell. "Hey," he repeated, now in front of me.

"Hi," I answered him. I stepped around him with the trash, but he stepped in front of me again, making us do this awkward little dance around each other. I don't know how he didn't get it through his head that I was working and didn't have time for his shit, but it didn't matter. We were talking, and that wasn't what I'd planned.

"You never called me."

"I never said I was going to," I answered him. I'd never once promised I would. I didn't think I'd even ever implied it, so I wasn't sure where he'd come to the conclusion that I might have picked up the phone unless he'd grossly misunderstood me kissing him. It didn't mean anything to me. It was solely a way to show him I'm actually not a shitty kisser and also that I was pissed off at him for saying otherwise. That's all it was, and he was acting like it was somehow more, like it was somehow something that would compel me to use his number.

"I was hoping you'd change your mind," he said. So, he *did* know. "How are you?"

"Working. Obviously." I didn't have time for the bullshit, but even as I kept trying to take the trash out, he continued to follow behind me like a lost puppy. "Aren't you going to go swim or something?" *Or do anything that isn't following me around.*

"You're still pissed at me." I don't know why it took him as long as it did to come to that conclusion, but he finally got there, and I wanted to praise the universe for him somehow eventually, finally figuring it out after I'd tried giving him every indication of it.

"Wow, what gave you that impression?" I asked him. I knew my voice was cold when I said it. I wasn't sure why he couldn't get the hint and drop it there.

"I'm sorry. I wasn't, uh, I wasn't trying to be shitty or anything. I wanted to...I don't know. I don't know what I was thinking at all. I'm sorry." He looked at his feet and I could tell he meant it, that he'd never meant to be as awful as he'd been. I swear it was the first time he'd ever been genuine and honest to me.

"You were trying to get my attention. You know what you did instead? You ruined any shot you could have possibly thought you had with me. Is that at least a little close to what you were thinking?" The way he hung his head and slumped his shoulders made it damn clear I was spot-on with my summary. "I'll be real with you, Tristan. I'm not interested. I wasn't interested before, but faking a drowning has got to be by far the worst way you could ever try to get my attention, okay? It was really fucking stupid of you. Maybe don't, I don't know, basically traumatize someone with their worst memories in life when you try to get in their pants, okay? Now, if you'll excuse me, I have actual work to get done." I sidestepped him again and heaved the trash into the dumpster and then turned to see he was still standing there. "By the way, James would probably be down to talk to someone who is willing to pull that kind of stunt. You should get his number." I nodded toward James.

"Okay," he said softly. He looked so small and defeated in that moment, like I'd ruined his life or something. I don't know. I was still really pissed off at him, but my stupid, stupid empathy was getting the best of me in a way that left me feeling almost bad for saying it. I mean, I wasn't empathetic enough to un-say it, but the way he acted was enough for me to feel guilty for advising him that direction. It wasn't that the two of them were a bad match. After all, they were both young, dumb, and...you know the rest. But the idea he was that upset about it left me feeling badly.

"You're not going to, are you?" I asked him. It was a stupid thing to ask, especially because the last thing I wanted to know was the answer, but I couldn't help myself. I asked him anyway.

"Probably not," he admitted.

"What do you have against him anyway?" I asked. I honestly wanted to know. I couldn't necessarily care any less about James. I didn't mind him hanging around me, but we weren't that close. I was more curious about what Tristan saw—or rather didn't see—in him that kept him so far away from James. Maybe James was right, even. Maybe Tristan's problem was that James was a guy, and maybe our kiss was sort of one of those, I don't know...things. A part of me even wondered if the drowning and kissing thing was some kind of dare. In all fairness, I might have disliked Tristan less if it *had* been a dare. Then I could have distributed my anger a little bit toward his friends, not just him.

But naturally, that's not what it was about. Instead, Tristan considered his words carefully, it seemed like. "He seems nice, okay? And he's cute or whatever, I don't know. But I like somebody else." He shrugged. "It'd be shitty to get his hopes up when I know I'd drop him in a heartbeat if the person I actually did like seemed down at all. That's it."

He flashed his eyes up at me, and it felt a little too obvious. "You know the person you like might not like you back, right? And then you missed out on James for no reason? I'm not trying to kill your dreams here, but it's always a possibility." If by any chance he was talking about me, I wanted to make it as clear as I could that I wasn't interested in the slightest. If it wasn't about me, then at least I'd said something, because given his special brand of annoying, there was a good chance anyone else he liked felt the same way about him I did. I figured I'd spell it out as a precautionary measure. "Besides, if you give him your number, you'll probably get laid." If emotional appeals didn't work, I figured that one would. If Tristan was stupid and horny enough to almost die to kiss me, I was pretty sure he was the breed of super-sex-desperate who would go for that reasoning and give James a chance.

"Yeah, okay. I guess I could talk to him." Tristan shrugged and turned away. "Thanks," he muttered under his breath, almost as if he didn't want me to hear it. He was definitely still upset. I wasn't blind enough to see that wouldn't work either, but it wasn't my problem. I had work to do. And the thing is, for some reason, I was dumb enough to believe the entire conversation there would be the end of it. But, of *course,* it wasn't. Why would it have been? My life didn't go that easily, ever. The second I saw James at work the next day, he was headed right for me and he was very, clearly, obviously pissed off.

"Why'd you have to go talk to him?" he demanded. "Couldn't you have just dropped it after he rejected me? You really think I needed two rejections to get the point?"

"What the hell happened?" How had we gone from where James was at first to where he was then? I hadn't the slightest idea. I shouldn't have asked. It wasn't my job to figure it out or deal with it, but suddenly I'd become Connor Molina, relationship therapist for these two. This was the sole reason I didn't hang out with baby gays like James. They could get really grating, really fast. If they would have just banged and gotten it over with, it would have been fine, but for some reason they both had some stupid idea that they needed to hook up with the right guy. The problem was, they also had different ideas about who the right guy for them was, and they couldn't get on the same damn page.

"He basically told me you said he should call me, which would have been great, but he followed it up with this bullshit about how he appreciated me being that into him, but that he also wished my friends wouldn't come to him about it, so now he's gone from being all 'cool but I'm not down' to thinking I'm some sort of idiot who can't get the hint."

Jesus, Tristan had a whole hell of a lot to learn about not going nuclear on things. Even if he didn't want James at that point, there was a very good chance in a small town like Springdale he'd want him later. Burning a bridge on someone when you haven't even slept with them yet is some real rookie shit.

"So, he thinks I told you to talk to him!" James flailed his arms in frustration, and I realized then that I hadn't been listening to a word he'd been saying for a solid three or four minutes.

"So now what? You want me to go clear shit up somehow, tell him you didn't say a word to me? That somehow I just came up with your attraction to him all on my own like some kind of flirting savant or something?" It was outlandish and I was clearly being sarcastic, which is why it seemed like no surprise that James took me quite literally.

"Yeah, that would be really helpful, actually. Right now, he thinks I'm super pushy. It fucking sucks, man. You ruined everything."

"Fine, okay." I was kicking myself for ever suggesting it. "Next time I see him, I'll tell him it wasn't you. I don't think it'll change a damn thing and suddenly make him want to hook up or something, but I'll say it if it's so important to you."

James just shrugged. "I have to get to work," he grumbled. "Do whatever." It had to have been obvious in my tone I didn't want to. High on the list of things that I never signed up for that summer was herding young gays and helping them learn to get laid without fucking it up. But you know, I guess that came with the territory, didn't it?

Chapter Six

I meant to talk to Tristan. Seriously, I did. I had given James my word, whether I actually wanted to get involved or not, and I meant to do it. But to be honest, going over and dealing with his bullshit also seemed like the least appealing part of my day. So, I didn't do it. This felt like one of those things James might just have to deal with. Disappointment happens. Shit happens. It shouldn't have been my problem to begin with anyway. It wasn't *my* fault James was hopelessly devoted and Tristan was a dumbass of epic proportions. But James kept glaring at me, and Tristan kept looking all wounded and shit and things that weren't my problem were clearly becoming my problem. I wanted to do my job, go home, work on my homework, and jack off. Was that really too much for me to ask?

Except clearly it was. While I was grabbing the things to clean the bathroom from the storage room, the door closed behind me. It was startling, but I first assumed it closed itself. I should have known better. Instead, I turned to find Tristan standing there. He'd followed me into the damn storage room for whatever reason. Part of me figured it was because James had said something, since he realized I wasn't really going to get around to it. Or maybe it was something else, I didn't fucking know. "Can we talk?"

"I'm at work," I reminded him. "I've got bathrooms to clean."

"Yeah, that sounds really fun," he said, voice dripping with sarcasm. "Anyway, it'll just take a second, and I don't think anyone's paying that much attention. Say you couldn't find the toilet cleaner if you have to, I don't know."

"Fine. What do you want?" I was realizing it would take me more time to argue with him than to do what he wanted in the first place and hear him out.

"What's your problem with me?"

"You mean outside of the part where you faked your death to kiss me without permission? I'd say that's reason enough to have issues with you."

"So, you're going to stay mad at me forever for that, or do you have some other reason to be all pissed off at me?" He asked the question like it was nothing, and for a second, I couldn't believe he was being serious. He was basically brushing everything off as if he didn't realize the way he'd acted for the first two weeks of the summer.

"What do you want from me, Tristan? You want me to stand here and tell you that you're right, and I was all wrong about you? That I'll call you every night before I fall asleep? Is that what you're after?" I rolled my eyes and tried to nudge past him, but he stood between me and the door. I wasn't trapped—I could have easily taken him even if he *was* bigger than me—but I also wasn't in the mood to fight him.

"I want you to tell me you didn't want to kiss me."

"I didn't want to kiss you," I said. My voice came out less convincing than I'd planned. It threw me off guard a little bit. For a moment, it sounded almost like I did want to do it. And I don't know. It's complicated. In hindsight, I can't quite sort through it all. Maybe a tiny part of me sort of did want to, not because I didn't think he was a total jerk, but because... I don't know why. I really can't explain it.

"Right, yeah, got it." I could see the wheels spinning with the way he started to smirk, and I swear to God, I wanted to shove him out of my way and get back to work. Except I didn't. Honestly? The bathroom could wait two seconds. "So, then it would be really, really easy for you to tell me you don't want to kiss me again, wouldn't it?"

This kid. This stupid fucking kid. I should have known from the beginning he was going to have a good time ruining my life. "I don't want to kiss you again," I said, but this time it was obvious how much I was lying. My body was betraying me, and I licked my lips. Something about how bold he was being, something in his intensity then had me intrigued about what he'd do and where he planned to take this. I didn't want him, and I definitely didn't like him, but a huge part of me was really, really curious about him. He was obviously playing to win. I like when people play to win.

"You don't?" he asked, stepping toward me. We weren't very far apart anymore. It would have taken me two steps to get into his space, to kiss him myself, to do whatever it was he wanted, but I couldn't bring myself to do that right away, not when I knew it was all part of whatever game he was playing. I didn't *want* him to win. At the same time, I absolutely did.

"No," I said, and then he took a step closer to me.

"Really? So, I don't have your permission?" he asked, turning my own words back on me.

Shit. Shit shit shit. Everything about the situation was ridiculous. And in a weird way, I loved that.

"I have to go," I said, my mouth suddenly dry and my willpower fading fast. "If I don't get the bathroom cleaned,

I'm going to lose my job." Yeah, I'm very aware of the fact I never answered his question. I think I was afraid that if I tried answering it, I'd answer it wrong.

"The door's jammed," he said, like it was some sort of dare. "Right? You're stuck in here because it's jammed? And you'll figure out how to get it unstuck in just a second, right? They really need to fix that door, don't they?" It took me a second to catch on, but when I did, I marveled at how convincing he was. It was enough to almost make me believe the door was stuck and I couldn't clean right then. I hated the fact I was damn near enchanted by his words when I was still that angry with him. And I was genuinely angry with him, don't get me wrong. In a lot of ways, this only served to make me angrier, but at the same time, it turned me on. That was incredibly dangerous.

"I don't have time for this," I said, but my words had lost all their power. I was giving in, and it was obvious. I hated myself for it.

"It isn't your fault the door is stuck," he suggested. "They should really take care of it more. Invest in some WD-40 or something."

"You're not supposed to be in here anyway," I protested weakly. "If they catch you in here, and they know I let you stay, I'll be fired."

"You didn't know I was in here, and the door jammed before you saw me," he suggested. "I won't let you get fired."

"You'll get kicked out of the pool for going in an employee-only area," I warned.

"Okay. So? I don't care. Let them kick me out. Let them ban me." He took another step toward me and then there wasn't any space between us. I could feel his breath against my mouth, and I was paralyzed. Part of me wanted to walk away and stop this kind of madness, but I couldn't. As much as that part of me wanted to say no, there was a louder part of me saying yes, yes, *God yes*. It didn't matter that I hated him and it didn't matter that I was being a horrible person knowing James was interested in him and it didn't matter that I was at work and everything about this was against the rules. I could worry about all of that later. Right now, it mattered that he was so close to me and I hadn't gotten laid in actual weeks and the wires in my brain between hatred and lust were crossed.

"Do I have your permission this time?" he asked.

I nodded, but before he could act on it, I took matters into my own hands, leaning in and kissing him. *Yes, it was stupid. Yes, it was probably going to seem like a massive mistake in hindsight*, I thought the second I did it. I was sure I was absolutely going to regret it.

But it was so, so good. His tongue against mine was startling, like my brain had said yes before my body contemplated what was happening. I almost dropped the bucket of cleaning supplies on his foot, but instead I pulled back long enough to set them down and let him have what he wanted, let him tug my lower lip between his teeth. He cupped a hand around the back of my head and put the other hand on my waist and turned me until I was backed up against the door. "See? It's jammed," he whispered, and then his lips were on my neck. If anyone caught us, I was thoroughly fucked, but in that moment it didn't matter. I couldn't have cared less about my job no matter how badly I needed it. Mostly because all the blood was rushing to my *other* head and...what was work anyway? I couldn't recall. He was kissing my collarbone and I wasn't wearing a shirt because it was hot that day anyway, and when he worked his way down, flicked his tongue over my nipple, I nearly lost it, coming unglued at how good it felt. He was trying to work his way lower, to get me to say okay, to take a whole hell of a lot longer than kissing would take. I was going to be gone for too long, and I was sure of it, my brain catching up to the rest of me and realizing this was such a bad idea.

"What are you doing?" I asked. My breath caught in my throat and my voice quivered. What the fuck *was* he doing, anyway, my brain kept wondering.

"I'm getting you un-mad at me," he said, his eyes flashing up to meet mine. His lips barely left my skin. When he spoke, I could feel the movement—he was *that* close.

"I'm still mad at you," I told him.

"Your dick says otherwise."

He was right. I couldn't control the physical response to my desire for him. I was hard, and it was painfully obvious in my bright-red guard shorts. His fingers were on my waistband, looped in as he looked up at me. I could have said no then. I could have stopped him and walked out of the supply room and I don't think he would have pushed it past that anymore. It would have all been over. I am 100 percent, completely, undeniably certain he would have dropped it and moved on and never spoken to me again that summer.

But I didn't. I gave him a small nod and it was all over. He was nuzzling at my length in my shorts, burying his face against it, kissing it through my swim trunks, and I was dying. It felt too good. Maybe if he'd caught me some other week, maybe if it hadn't been so long since I'd gotten some, maybe I wouldn't have responded the way I did.

But he did catch me at a weak moment, and I did give in.

He tugged my shorts down, not all the way, but enough so one of his hands could hold them in place around my upper thighs as his other hand set to work on taking care of my need. If we got caught, both of us would have been way more than fucked, but it felt like, somehow, we could have denied it if I wasn't all the way undressed. Not that we could have denied it, but at the time, my brain was fuzzy, and this seemed like a good idea.

He was an expert with his tongue, far better at that than he was at even kissing me. When he worked me with his mouth, it made everything blurry and confusing. I wanted it, wanted more, wanted everything. I loved how it felt to have his mouth on me, the wet warmth surrounding me, the sound of it, the way he grasped my thigh harder. But then he let the shorts fall and grabbed my ass with both of his hands to take me deeper, deeper until I was hitting the back of his throat. His eyes watered when he looked at me, and for some reason, that was the hottest thing. I didn't want to choke him, not by any means, but I really wanted to feel him and let him feel me. He swallowed when I was in that deep, and I could feel the movement of his throat around me. When he pulled off me, it was painfully obvious I was close.

That was for the best. I didn't have time to last long here. Any other time, sure, I might have tried to make myself last longer, but I was at work. I was missing in action when I should have been cleaning the bathroom. So, I didn't stop myself, letting it happen.

"I'm gonna come," I told him, and he smiled. He liked the way he had me wrapped around his finger in that moment, and as he leaned back, let the tip rest on his tongue, he used his hand, jerking me over the edge until it landed on his tongue. If I wasn't already coming hard, I would have come all over again seeing that, to be honest. The sight of him like that still rattles in my brain, still sticks there when I'm playing solo and need a good memory to help me out.

I may have been dealing with the worst summer of my life, but on the bright side, I'd gotten a damn good blowjob out of it. As he tugged my shorts back up, he kept me against the door, a hand on either side of me, keeping me there as he leaned in to kiss me. I could taste myself all over his lips and tongue and I was a little bit angry with myself for letting it happen. "Are you still mad at me?" he asked, but his voice was low this time, less forceful and commanding now he'd gotten what he wanted.

"Yes," I said, but there wasn't an ounce of power behind the word.

"You going to call me?"

I desperately wanted to say no, to tell him to go fuck himself, to remind him I was still positively furious with him. But dammit, he gave good head, and I couldn't seem to remember what had me quite so angry in the first place. I could remember, sure, but I also didn't get why it had all seemed so important to me. I looked at him, considering my options, and then I answered, "Maybe."

Chapter Seven

"You were in the supply room for a long time." With the entire staff there, anyone could have noticed I was missing. Maria, Jess, hell, even my manager Greg. But no. Of course, none of them noticed I was gone for twenty minutes longer than I should have been. Instead, it had to be James who recognized how long it took me in the supply closet. Of course. That was the story of my life, especially my life that summer.

"The door jammed. Haven't you seen how it sticks? I was stuck in there and totally freaking out," I told him.

"I haven't noticed."

"Oh." Fuck. "Well, it does. They need to get some WD-40 or something on it," I said, repeating Tristan's words. "Anyway, I'm back now. What do you need?" I don't know why I copped an attitude with him. I was gone way longer than I should have been. But now I was cleaning a toilet and I needed to get it done without James hovering over me during his break.

"I wanted to ask if you ever got a chance to talk to Tristan." I wondered if he'd seen Tristan leave the supply room a couple of minutes after me, like we'd planned, but I didn't think he'd noticed. Instead, I got the impression this was a stab in the dark to see if I was hooking up with Tristan. Or maybe I just felt called out and convicted because that's exactly what I'd been doing. Most likely he was asking because I'd promised him I would a week before and still hadn't done it.

"No," I said. "I'm sorry. I seriously meant to, but I've barely seen him." Lying wasn't my usual style. To be honest, it wasn't even in my style to lie about it when I hooked up with someone a friend of mine was into. Honesty was a better policy. Not that I made a habit of hooking up with people my friends were into or anything, but you know, if it happened at some point. I'm not the spineless guy who lies about that sort of thing at all, but something about James and how he was...I don't know, how he was the way he was, I guess...made me not want to tell him the truth, not right then. Not at work. So, I lied through my teeth. "If I see him around, I'll tell him, okay?"

"You know what? Forget it. He's probably forgotten by now anyway."

"Yeah, you know, probably. I mean, I don't really know him, but who holds onto something for that long? He probably moved on, especially if he's interested in some other dude," I told him.

"We don't know it's another dude," he reminded me. I tried not to let on that I knew the person he was into was another guy. I knew that because it was me. Obviously. But the blush burned through me, all-consuming, and I was terrified it was apparent to anyone, especially James.

"Right. Anyway, I'm almost done in here. You want to snag Jess and have her get the bucket for the girls' room?" I needed James to go away. I needed space so I could sort out what I was thinking without him hovering. I had hoped to use the time in the bathroom to remind myself I was royally fucking up by letting Tristan have an inch (or six and a half of them, to be exact), because he'd clearly take a mile if I let him have any more. I could tell I was taking a bad summer and turning it into a worse one. I needed the time to give myself a pep talk so I could remind myself to shut shit down. Instead, James had gabbed at me the entire time and I was frustrated. I hadn't gotten any time to think, to convince myself how stupid it was to get sucked into this.

"Yeah, okay," James said, breaking my focus.

But he had left me alone with only one toilet left to clean, and that wasn't anywhere near enough time for me to figure everything out. It also didn't help that after I left the bathroom, I was back on my stand. That should've been fine, being on stand. I could have typically still thought about stuff even while I was watching, but no. Tristan had to come over into my section. He *had* to. And it wasn't like he'd come over just to swim, because whatever, if he was swimming, that was fine. I could have checked and made sure he wasn't drowning or whatever, since he had a habit of trying to do that, apparently, without having to pay too much attention. No, he had to come and be an idiot right in front of me. Again.

He got right in front of my chair and started doing handstands and shit like a child. That was fine until he almost kicked an actual child, which meant I was blowing my whistle at him, and that would have been fine, too, but he was all "what?" like because I let him suck my dick, suddenly rules somehow didn't apply to him anymore.

"You almost kicked her," I said, shouting at him, and he swam closer to me now that I was off my stand and standing by the edge of the pool.

"Sorry. I wasn't trying to hurt anybody."

"Yeah, okay," I shrugged and tried to stifle the obvious annoyed look on my face. "Just be careful." I didn't have time for this. I didn't have time for him to think there were exceptions now, that anything had changed between us. He leaned up on the lip of the pool, dripping water all over my feet now I was standing at the edge. Then I felt him put a hand on my foot too. I didn't try to move, but I did look at him, trying to figure out what his angle was here. Was he trying to fuck with me? Did he just want to touch me?

"What are you doing?" I asked.

"Nothing," he said, but he didn't try to move away. He looked up my body, making eye contact, and if he'd been a few feet higher up my body instead of at my feet, it would have given me flashbacks to what had happened an hour before, I swear. This was already fucking with my head in the worst ways.

"I'm working," I said, thinking maybe being firm would help the situation. Maybe he'd get the hint that it was a one-off thing, I thought, not something we'd do again. The whole thing he'd wanted was for me not to be mad at him anymore, and fine, whatever. I wasn't as pissed off as I'd been previously. But he'd accomplished that goal and it was over.

"What time are you off?"

"What does it matter?" I asked.

"I'm just curious," he said. Then he bit his lip. For all the times I'd wanted to shove his sorry ass back into the water, that was the time I wanted to do it the most. This wasn't happening. We weren't ever supposed to hook up the first time, and the last thing I needed was for us to repeat the whole situation. But the stupid, stupid jerk had to press his luck.

"Go be curious somewhere else," I said. I figured eventually he'd have to get the hint, to understand that it wasn't happening. We were definitely, completely not hooking up again. Ever.

"Okay, later," he said, winking at me. God, the audacity of him, honestly. He swam off as if the entire exchange had never happened. If I had to make a list of the most infuriating human beings I've met in my life, he would be at the top of it without question. But the thing that made me angrier than how he acted during my shift was how he acted after. I had planned to switch off after the day I'd had, to grab my shit out of my locker, go home, forget any of it ever happened. But Tristan couldn't let that happen. He couldn't drop it. As soon as I came out of the office, he was there.

"You off?"

"What's it matter?" I asked him, and honestly, what did it matter anyway? It wasn't like I was inviting him to come back to my place or anything.

"You're not sticking around to swim?" he asked. That afternoon was one of the rare evenings where I was scheduled to leave well before the pool closed, so it isn't like I wouldn't have had the time. And the thing is, Tristan was completely calling me out. I'm on the goddamn swim team, and so far that summer, I'd barely done any actual swimming. Unless I counted saving him from not-drowning, the most water I'd touched outside of hot showers was during lifeguard swim. I spent all that time in the lazy river, basically. I was being lazy, and he was calling me on it. Not that he knew he was, but he was.

"Oh, yeah, sure. That's what everyone wants to do with their time off. Stay at work longer. Thanks." I didn't mean to snap at him, but around him, it was almost instinctive. I know I can be a crummy person, and in that moment, I was definitely all-in on being a jerk. I knew I should have been in the lap pool after work, and it was what I'd planned to do when I'd gotten the job in the first place. Instead, my lazy ass was dead set on going home to play FIFA and jack off. I wanted to relax. Sue me.

"I was just askin'," he said. "You know you don't have to be so mad all the time." It wasn't the first time he'd called me out on being grumpy, and I knew it wouldn't be the last. All I wanted was to go home.

"Sorry," I muttered. I was almost sincere. "I'm going home."

"Oh. Okay. You working tomorrow?" I was half surprised when he didn't suggest following me or joining me for a while, coming home. After I'd gone off on him, I guess it made sense for him not to be that bold.

"I work every day." It was true. Aside from the couple of days I'd taken off after he'd fake-drowned, I'd worked every day of the summer, seven days each week. I didn't take days off if I could avoid it. For one, being alone with my thoughts was always a bad idea, and for two, I needed the money. Being a lifeguard didn't pay a ton, and I had rent, utilities, all of that. I was lucky I didn't need a second job just to keep my head above the metaphorical water, but it wasn't exactly like I was living in the best part of town. I lived in a shitty-ass apartment, still do. I make it work. All summer long, I was at the pool every day because I had to be. "Anyway, I gotta go," I told him. I didn't have anywhere in particular to be. I just didn't want him getting the impression I was there to chat whenever he felt like it.

"Cool. See you tomorrow, then," he said, giving a small wave.

"Yeah, all right. See you around." Whatever, I figured. I'd let him keep his hopes up for another encounter with me. I figured I had more willpower than that. I was certain it wasn't going to happen again, but I also didn't see the point in killing his hopes and dreams. Maybe he even figured I'd somehow reciprocate or something, return the favor for what he'd done for me earlier in the day, but I rolled my eyes. I figured he would have been delusional to think that, but I couldn't know what he was thinking.

Chapter Eight

I was beyond annoyed with myself when I woke up hard as a rock. I'd overslept, which already meant I was going to be late if I wasn't careful, hurrying through the morning. Waking up hard wasn't an issue. Waking up hard when I couldn't handle it? That sucked. I'd dreamed about what happened at the pool. That sounds so stupid, especially because the last thing I'd wanted was for anything like that to happen again, but I did dream about it. I dreamed about him sucking me off in the supply room, and I could perfectly picture his lips wrapped around me, how good thrusting in felt, my back against the door so no one could enter, head spinning from how he'd hollow his cheeks a little bit as he pulled back. Ugh. The dream was enough to drive me insane. I hated the fact I liked it so much. I had a class to get through, one that needed focus I didn't have. I couldn't even jerk off in the shower because there wasn't time left for a shower before I had to leave.

Of course, my roommate had to say shit about it too. "Running late today?" God, he was annoying. When you get stuck hanging around for the summer at the last minute, you don't exactly get your choice of roommates. It wasn't like I'd picked Alex. He'd simply been the only person left who I thought I could survive living with for the next year. Most of the time, he was fine. When I was late and horny, not so much.

"Obviously," I snapped at him, stuffing my books into my bag.

"Looks like you've got a little unfinished business there," he said, nodding at the crotch of my sweatpants. My damn boner hadn't calmed down yet that morning, because the harder I tried not to think about the dream, the more the thought was at the forefront of my mind, and the more my reaction kept inconveniently reappearing physically.

"Yeah, got it," I said. "Later." I kicked myself for somehow picking up the use of Tristan's favorite farewell greeting. Instead of slinging my bag over my shoulder, I carried it in front of me, trying to hide the evidence of my filthy, impure, stupid thoughts. Not filthy or impure because of any other reason than I was thinking of *Tristan*. Ugh. There wouldn't be time to take care of the issue after class, either, not when I had to get to work. I cursed myself for sleeping through my alarm, and I considered the ramifications of handling what I needed while I drove. Unfortunately, that seemed way too risky, so I pressed on and prayed I'd have a few minutes somewhere in my schedule to find release.

The thing is, I didn't. Class dragged on, and I got held up after it talking to the professor about an assignment. I get that no one could have known I was desperate to get off in the nearest bathroom, and obviously I couldn't have told anyone, but my focus wasn't on what he was saying, and it felt like anyone who could put a barrier between me and my hopeless attempt to get off, did. I wanted to scream. Driving to the pool wasn't any easier, feeling myself throbbing and aching for anything. Blue balls were such a bitch. I was craving a chance to get it taken care of, but the second I got there, I was on duty and working.

"Hey." Tristan swam up and propped himself on the side of the pool at my feet.

"Hey," I said, doing everything I could not to look at him. I was terrified if I looked down at him, I'd feel the same desperate stirring in the pit of my stomach again, and right now I needed to focus on other things. My need was his damn fault for being decent at giving head, and that's what it all boiled down to. If he hadn't been any good at it, none of this would have happened. After dreaming about him the night before, I wanted to kick myself for starting to sort of, kind of agree with James that yes, in the right light, when his hair was dripping with water, and his body was tan and glistening and whatever other cheesy words I could use to describe how he looked, Tristan was maybe, possibly, a little tiny bit more attractive than I'd wanted to give him credit for. So, because of that, I couldn't look at him. I couldn't.

"How are you, pretty boy?" he teased, and a quick glance down showed he was joking, that he didn't mean to annoy me with it. "Connor?" he tacked on—I think in case I felt like he went too far.

"I'm fine." I gritted my teeth. I needed desperately for him to go the fuck away so I could focus on my job. If he wasn't careful, I was going to pop a boner right then and there.

"You look good today," he said.

"Thanks." He was flirting. The thing is, a part of me, a big one, wanted to give in. I thought if I flirted back, he might do what he did again, the thing I'd said I was done with. I knew if I flirted back, he'd probably get me off and it was probably worth being nice to him, but I was trying to work, trying to scan the water, trying to do all of that. Every time he talked to me, he diverted my focus away from my job. I would flash back to what we'd done in the supply room.

"You're quiet," he told me.

"Dang it, Tris, I'm working. I can't sit here and chat you up while I'm trying to make sure no one pretends to drown on me," I said, annoyance written all over my face.

"Ooh, a nickname for me. Tris. I like it." I hadn't even realized I'd nicknamed him anything. I was just trying to say what I said, and I had shortened his name in the process. Not that my intent mattered. He'd taken it as some sort of sign of affection. "Anyway, see you around." He swam off and I looked down at where he had been. Aside from a few waves lapping at the side of the pool, it was like he'd never been there at all.

Time dragged. My break ended up starting late because of a minor emergency with a water filter, and when I finally got the filter fixed, I was pretty sure I was literally dying from horniness. Break times were only fifteen minutes, but a guy could do a lot in fifteen minutes, especially if he had a little bit of help. It wasn't hard to catch Tristan's eye, to nod toward the bathrooms. I closed us in and then pushed him against the wall with a bruising kiss. I'm not kidding—the kiss was so intense it almost hurt a little. I was too desperate to slow down, too needy. I hate being that kind of guy. Usually, I'm more restrained. In hindsight, I should have been more restrained there too.

"Can you suck my dick again? I only have fifteen minutes." I know I was asking a lot. He'd already sucked me off once without any kind of reciprocation offered on my part, but he sank to his knees willingly without bringing the fact up or complaining.

"Honestly thought you'd never ask," he said, wasting no time with the lead-up he'd done in the storage room. Today, he didn't kiss my stomach or my thighs. Instead, he got down there, slid my shorts down, and kissed the length before taking me deep. Today, he was wet and sloppy, the noise of his saliva on my skin sounding so, so good. "Tastes like chlorine," he mumbled. I tried not to roll my eyes. I hadn't been in the pool that high up. I started close to finishing, genuinely from the second he got his mouth on me. My hands were on the back of his head, and I was relishing every flick of his tongue. God, I felt so much need right then. I could have come so easily, could have finished all over his face, I was so close. Jesus, I was close.

"Connor? You in here? Somebody hit their head and we need a concussion check." Meg was shouting and there was no way I could pretend I didn't hear, not when someone was hurt. Tristan knew what her call meant, too, and he stopped immediately, tugging my shorts up.

"Go," Tristan told me, standing up. "I'll get you off later if you want."

I felt badly for not doing anything to help him out, for not even offering, so I pulled him close and kissed him. "Thanks. See you later?"

And then it was back to work. I hadn't even gotten a full break, and I was wondering how I could be the only lifeguard on duty who knew proper concussion protocol. I get that I was the only one studying any sort of medicine. No one else had even started college, so it made sense, but I didn't get why Greg couldn't have done the check. I glanced up and he was dealing with a kid who had a nosebleed. Right, he could only clear one emergency at a time.

Instead, I was out there, sitting down next to the injured girl, taking care of things. God, I should've been the manager. "Okay, look at me, let me see your eyes," I said softly to her. "Can you keep your eyes open for me? I know it's bright, but I really need you to look at me, okay?" Her pupils dilated fine, but she seemed unfocused, like she was confused or worried. "Is your mom here?"

"She dropped me off," she said.

"Okay. Tell me about school, okay? What grade are you going into?" I was trying hard to get her to make small talk. I knew she was probably concussed, but she was holding her head still, and I wanted to be sure everything was okay.

"I'll be in third grade," she told me, holding arms across her stomach. I felt around her neck, trying to make sure nothing felt off, but everything looked fine.

"That sounds really fun. Third grade is exciting. So, you'll be in a new school soon, then, right?" In Springdale, anyone third grade and up moved to another building, and giving her more to talk about seemed to make her feel calm.

"Yeah," she said. She closed her eyes again.

"Are you dizzy at all?"

"A little bit."

"Does your head hurt?" I asked her.

"Yeah. It hurts right here." She pointed, and I gently rubbed at the side of her head. I could feel the knot under her hair. It was definitely going to bruise over.

"All right, buddy. Since you're dizzy and you had a pretty hard knock on the head, I want you to be extra safe. We're going to call your mom, okay? I want you to come sit in the office with me while we wait for her."

"Am I gonna be okay?" Her voice was small and quivering, like she was scared, and I wanted to slap her mom for dropping such a young child off at the pool without supervision. Parents acted as if we were babysitters, like they didn't know any given guard could be watching over a section with fifty patrons swimming. We couldn't be everyone's babysitter all the time, even if we tried. And, yeah, I actually fucking tried.

"I think you're going to be just fine. Don't worry. I want to make sure you do me a big favor, though, okay? I want you to go home and get lots of rest. Go easy on the TV and tablet for a few days, all right?" With the possible concussion, her brain needed the rest. I just hoped she'd listen after she left the pool.

"Okay," she said, nodding. She seemed to be scared out of her mind, and she put her hand in mine, so small, and let me lead her to the front office check-in area. Thankfully, she didn't seem to need any sort of hospitalization. She was shaken, but not severely hurt. Calling her mom went quickly enough. I realized as we waited that I couldn't thank Tristan, or keep him up on what was happening, because I wouldn't see him until well after her mom got there. Instead, I tried to brush off the lingering thought of wanting to talk to him about it, or about whatever, and focused on what the little girl was telling me. She talked about her favorite movies, her favorite subject in school, and about her dog Tony. I listened to her talk for well over an hour before her mom finally showed up.

"I was getting groceries on the other side of town. What happened?" She demanded answers as if she hadn't taken over an hour to get here when I'd made it clear her daughter was hurt over the phone.

I started with, "I think she's going to be okay." If I were her parent, that's the thing I'd want to know first: prognosis and then details, not the other way around. "She had a pretty bad knock to the head, and she has a knot, but there's no cut and she's not bleeding or anything. I don't think she needs to go to the hospital at all, but you might want to make sure she rests a lot, maybe limit her screen time to give her head time to heal. She should feel better tomorrow." Her mother didn't say anything, so I kept talking. "You can put ice on the knot if it's bothering her and give her some children's ibuprofen or something if she says her head hurts at all." In that moment, I was thankful I had some sort of medical training. Any of the other guards would have likely replied with a shrug in terms of what to do or what happened. I know for sure James would have.

Her mother rolled her eyes. "I don't get why someone wasn't watching her," she said, shaking her head. "None of this would have happened if she had been watched in the first place." That part pissed me off. I get that kids come and go from pools all the time, but the pool also says they need supervision. It's on the sign, even, that parents should supervise their kids. Parents treat us like we're some kind of daycare center and we aren't. I couldn't have told you at a glance who was a latchkey kid who needed a place to go for the afternoon versus who had a mom who wanted to day drink and watch soap operas. That wasn't my job. Kids would come and go, and obviously as a lifeguard, my goal was always to make sure they played safe and left the pool in one piece, but for her to accuse me—hell, us—of not watching her kid when she was on the other side of town doing whatever the fuck she wanted with her afternoon? It was really rich of her, is all I was saying.

"We keep a very close watch on all of the kids here, ma'am," I told her. "Accidents happen though. If you've got the impression that we're not keeping a close enough eye on her, my advice would be to bring her to the pool yourself and see how we do, and also keep an eye on her. We keep track of pool safety. We don't babysit." I wasn't fucking around, and I definitely wasn't in the mood for her bullshit.

"I'd like to speak to the manager," she demanded. Yeah, it was safe to say she got the point of what I was telling her, that if she wanted to make sure her kid was safe, she could get off her lazy, selfish ass and watch her herself. But there wasn't a chance in hell Greg would talk to her. He had a policy about that: go into the office, try to "find" him, walk back and pretend we couldn't, and then give them his phone number instead. Most of the time, they'd never bother to call, so I did exactly that and went through the motions.

"He's busy tending to some training over what we can learn from this situation," I lied. "I've got his card here if you'd like to give him a call."

"He *will* be hearing about your attitude," she said, capping off her whole outrage with that quick remark. *Let her call him.* I didn't care. If she happened to get me fired, I'd be fucked, but that would be better than her yelling at me when I'd done the best I could. And honestly, there were a million reasons I should have been fired anyway. This wasn't one of them but being fired over it would have been cosmic justice.

I was angry with myself for getting all hot and heavy with Tristan at work. Even if I wasn't supposed to be watching on break, sometimes I still kept my eyes on the water, and I might have been able to do something, you know? I was frustrated that I'd put my own needs or wants over what was best for the patrons there, but I was also pissed at my coworkers that no one had seen her until it was too late. Worse, I was really angry with her mother for dropping off someone going into third grade. She wasn't even ten yet, and she was expected to know how to fend for herself at the pool. I shouldn't have let myself get angry at taking a break—I couldn't be switched on at all times for an entire summer. I had to get breaks.

"Okay, ma'am. When you call him, please let him know it was Connor you spoke to. I don't want any other guards getting reprimanded for our interaction." I turned my attention to the little girl then, ignoring her mother completely. "Hey, make sure you get some rest, okay? And put ice on it. Oh, and give Tony a big hug for me when you get home. I'm sure he'll help you heal up really fast."

Her mother could accuse us of not watching her child closely enough if she wanted to, but no one could ever accuse me of not giving a shit about the patrons at the pool, no matter how badly I hated my job. "Thanks, Connor. See you tomorrow," the little girl said, turning and giving a small wave. I wanted to high five her for proving my point to her mother—I actually cared a lot.

"See you tomorrow, buddy," I told her.

Chapter Nine

By the end of my shift, my balls were literally aching. I mean, throbbing kind of aching. It was bad enough when I woke up hard, but with Tristan getting me close and me not getting to finish, that was torture. Edging was definitely not my strong point or my personal kink. It was more like my personal hell. I thought about it nonstop during the rest of my shift, and no matter how many times I told myself I would have been stupid to do what I was wanting to do, my balls kept convincing me otherwise. By the end of the shift, I no longer had good reasons to talk myself out of it, which is why that evening, when my shift was over, I found myself standing against the wall by the drinking fountain, mentally willing Tristan to come over and talk to me. I mean, I obviously wasn't sick enough to walk up to him where anybody could see, but if he happened to walk by me, offer to fuck around or something, then I could say yes without it seeming like that was what I was doing, right?

It only took three minutes.

"You on break?" he asked me, pretending to get a drink from the drinking fountain. "Don't worry. He's on the other side of the pool. He won't see you talk to me."

"Who won't?"

"James. That's what you're worried about, right? That he's going to be all pissed off if we talk since he's into me." I'll give Tristan one thing. He could be cocky as all get-out, and I was really into it.

"Yeah. Anyway, I'm not on break. I'm off work."

"So why are you standing here, then? I thought you liked going home after your shift's over." He was calling me out on my bullshit, dragging up my past excuse to avoid him, and I was second-guessing things for a moment. He wasn't worth so much drama. But holy shit, I needed to get off, and he was the best ticket to that station.

"Not my fault you left some things unfinished in that bathroom," I said. I figured if I spun it around on him, made him feel like this was on him for not getting me off fast enough, maybe he'd offer to take care of my need for me.

"Mm, and that means you want what from me?" he asked, as if he didn't know exactly what I was asking, and as if he didn't know I was already swallowing my pride a lot to say as much as I had. I hated the idea of begging.

"If I need to spell it out for you, forget it," I said. I didn't have time for games, never mind that I was playing some myself. If he wasn't offering, I wasn't about to ask him. I'd already said more than I'd wanted to. I was hoping he'd walk up, ask if I was down, and then we'd get out of there, but he'd thrown me off, mentioning James, asking me what I wanted. Here's the thing. I don't ask for it. Me asking him in the bathroom was more than I ever resort to most of the time, so this was a lot bigger an issue for me. I can get sex just fine when I want it, without having to ask. I like nonverbal cues. But I hadn't been focused on getting laid. It wasn't that I couldn't get what I wanted. It was that I hadn't been trying and I was off my groove. Him asking me to ask was too much. I did the sane thing. I walked away and got in my car.

Except then he yanked the passenger door open and sat down beside me. "You want to do this?"

"Yeah," I said.

"Ask me nicely." I had no idea how I'd let what was essentially some stupid kid boss me around like that, make demands like he did, but I was desperate, and my need was evident.

"Please, Tristan," I said quietly. It was all I felt like I was willing to give. God, I hated him.

"Please what?"

"Please fuck me," I mumbled. If anyone had been listening in without context, they probably couldn't have made out the words, but Tristan knew.

"Yeah, okay," he said, and we sat in silence the rest of the way until I pulled up to my apartment. We didn't need to talk. I didn't need to get to know him. That's not what this was. This was sex. I needed to get off, and he was offering to help. He wasn't some new best friend or boyfriend or whatever else. He was sex. Nothing more.

I swear I half-dragged him up the stairs to my third-floor walk-up when I got there and tugged him through the living room without a lot of introduction. "Who's that?" Alex asked, and if he hadn't, I wouldn't have bothered saying anything at all.

"Tristan, that's Alex, Alex, Tristan," I barked out before I had the door closed. I backed Tristan up onto the double bed, pushed him onto it, and straddled him as I kissed him. With both of us still in swim trunks and nothing else, it made everything a whole hell of a lot easier. I could get my mouth on his chest, could get my teeth on his nipples, and make him groan. I hadn't done anything at all for him up until that point, so in a way it seemed like I threw him off a little bit, giving instead of just taking. I wanted to say something, to be all, *yeah, bitch, I can reciprocate,* but I didn't. I just kept working his chest with my tongue.

"Jesus, Connor, that feels amazing," he said, squirming under my every touch, melting like butter with each movement of my lips against his body. As I worked my mouth down his abs, I got it. I understood how every guard at the pool could think he was attractive. For the very first time, his sexiness was completely crystal clear to me. He was fitter than he looked, muscles revealing themselves as he breathed in, letting me run my tongue from his waistband up to his belly button, following the trail of brown hair there. I needed to get off, but he was enjoying the tease and I was enjoying his reaction to it.

I thought there might be a chance he'd come way too early when I started to kiss and lick over his swim trunks. He was hard, and as I worked my mouth along his length, he groaned. "Oh my God, Connor, please..." He didn't have to tell me please *what* because I knew what he wanted. Right then, I was more than happy to give him that, pulling his trunks down and getting up close and personal.

"Holy shit, you're huge," I said. I hadn't anticipated how big he'd be, how impressive his length would be underneath the cocky attitude and unchecked ambition to get with me. I mean, obviously his skill at giving head was enough that I wanted him again, but this...it wasn't what I'd anticipated, not really. A huge part of me needed him, needed to feel what he had to offer in that department. He was a good two inches bigger than me and my mind was racing.

"I know," he told me. I swear if I weren't dying to have him in me, I would have kicked him out of my bed for being so cocky, but honestly? I liked that he could hold his own. I had two years on him of age and experience and he still thought he could come in here and talk to me like he was hot shit and I was, for whatever reason, eating it up.

I got what he was saying now, the thing about me tasting like chlorine. He tasted like it too. I could sense the dried pool water on his skin from his swim earlier, and as I ran my tongue along him, his hands tangled in my hair. When he pulled the strands, I got even more turned on. He wanted me, and for once, that only made me want him more. I hated being so into everything he was doing.

When he was hard and dripping, I decided it was my turn to get what I wanted, and I kept him there with my hand while I worked my way back up his body with my mouth. "You should fuck me," I told him. Then I kissed him below his ear. I could feel how slick he was as I flicked my thumb over the tip of his cock. He wanted to fuck me too.

"You want...you want me to fuck you?" For a moment, he seemed surprised, like my cold standoffishness would somehow automatically mean I'd only want to top. But he was big, and I desperately wanted to feel every bit of it.

"Fuck yes, I do." I wasn't usually that enthusiastic, and perhaps if I'd been less sex-starved I would have shown more restraint then. But I was already hard, and I didn't even give him time to blow me. I needed it immediately, standing up and dropping my trunks on the floor. I didn't have the energy to second-guess what I was saying to him, what I was offering up out of lust and desperation.

"Okay. On the bed, all fours," he told me. Somehow, he thought since I was offering to take it, he was calling the shots. It was ridiculous, and I wanted to set him straight on that, to make it clear I was in charge still, but the idea wasn't a bad one, so I did it anyway. I figured he was ready. Hell, I knew he was ready because I'd gotten him there. But he knew what he was doing, getting behind me, up close and personal, and burying his face between my cheeks. He ate ass like a starving man, and I could feel every breathy groan as he pushed his nose against me to try to lick all the way down and back up. He'd barely breathe to really get in there, his whole face against me, trying to get deeper. I've been with some guys, all right? Nobody had ever made me feel the way he did, the way he got in there and really went for it.

The rimjob was almost torture. Not because it didn't feel good—it felt mind-blowingly awesome—but because I really felt like I was about to bust, and he still hadn't fucked me. It was all I wanted, for him to fuck me, for him to get all up on me and in me and grab my shoulder as he pounded me like the weak little bitch I can be for that kind of thing. I'm a slut for a big cock and his was amazing. So, between my breathlessness and my "oh God, yeah," and "don't stop, that feels so good," at some point I had to be like "okay, enough, please fuck me." Thankfully, he was ready for that too. He nodded toward the bedside table. "Condom's in there?"

I nodded. "And lube."

I can't even explain how good he was then, how amazing it felt after all the lead-up, the waiting, the desperation all day to feel him push into me. Honestly, it's a wonder I didn't make a mess of the striped sheets from his initial thrust alone. But I didn't, and he kept going, and he fucked me good. I mean, I've had incredible sex before, but something about what Tristan was doing got to me. The way he put his hands on my neck for leverage, the way he kissed my shoulder when he'd hit me nice and deep with it...it sounds cheesy as fuck to say I was seeing stars, but I can't think of another way to explain it, to convey how good it was. And yeah, maybe some of it was just waiting from the time I'd woken up to get dicked down, but I think a lot of it was also that he was really, really good at fucking.

"I'm so close," I groaned. I was almost babbling outside of that, so it was a miracle I was even forming coherent words at that point.

"Say my name when you do?" It felt like a very weird, specific thing to ask, strange he'd ask when I was so ready to come. "Call me Tris," he said, kissing my neck, his body draped over mine. I didn't know if he somehow needed the ego boost, the knowledge that I was saying how good the sex was, that it was *him* fucking me specifically, whatever, but it was something.

"God, Tris, I'm gonna come, I'm...fuck, yeah, like that, you're fucking me so good, Tris," I said, and then I was coming and he was coming and it all sort of blurred together as he was lying down on my back and cradling me in his arms. I felt amazing, felt overwhelmed, and whether I felt the sensation in that moment or not, I knew it was coming, and eventually it did: I felt sore.

Chapter Ten

I'm not entirely sure that he grasped the full concept at first, got the picture that this was just sex. He didn't necessarily try anything, you know? He didn't reach for my hand or whatever, but he put his hand on my knee on the way back to the pool, like there might be a chance he'd either go for my hand or snake his way up my leg until he was at my dick. Which, Jesus, how insatiable was he? I thought I was an absolute horndog half the time, but for him to go for my cock again that fast, it was something else. The pool was long closed by the time I got him back there and his car was the only one in the lot.

It seemed weird to wait for him to open his door in silence, to let him out without saying *something,* so I did. "Why do you hang out here all the time?" I asked him. The pool had our regulars—we called them the pool rats—but most of them were younger, middle school or whatever. He was the oldest of the people who were there every single day. Even his friends weren't there as often as he was, instead coming on a steady rotation, some friends one day, other friends the next.

"I don't know," he said. "Gets me out of the house, I guess." I couldn't place the tone of his voice, couldn't tell if the statement was coming from boredom or from hurt.

"Not a fan of your house, I take it?"

"Nah. I mean, I'm going to the community college here in the fall. It'll be a lot easier if I stay home, cheaper than getting a place, you know? It's...it's just a pain in the ass to be there sometimes. I don't know." He looked out of the window and rested his chin on his hand as he leaned against the door. He didn't move to get out of the car at all.

"Sucks living at home when you're nineteen, huh? Listening to your parents' rules and stuff?" I could relate to that a little bit, at least. The summer after my freshman year was difficult. I mean, I know I'd been itching to go home over this last summer instead of staying for summer classes, but I got the reality that it was an adjustment, especially after college or something. You're an adult, but you're not. You have rules and responsibilities like you're a kid, but you've got the age and desire for freedom any adult has. Even if I wanted to be at home for the summer, there were perks to spending a summer away from it. Downside: living here was more expensive, and I had to work all summer to pay for freedom, which wasn't even freedom because of class and the job. Upside: the obvious stuff like the idea I could fuck whenever I wanted without having to work sex around my parents' schedule. If we'd met back home, I wouldn't have been able to sleep with him any time I wanted. Not that I could over the summer anyway, since I had work, but you get the idea. What I mean is, at home, I would've had to save it for a time when they were at work or it was their date night. I couldn't just bring him over out of nowhere. Here, I didn't need permission for us to be alone.

"It's, uh. It's complicated," Tristan told me. "My dad isn't super okay with, I don't know...when he's not super accepting of me as a person, it's easier not to be there. Sometimes it feels like he thinks he can fix or change me, but if he doesn't see me, he can't...whatever. It's really complicated," he said again, and it hurt to hear him talk about it. He moved his hand that was against his face, rubbed his eyes with it like he was tired or something. "I should get home anyway. He'll probably be askin' where I was."

He moved to open the door, but I reached out, put my hand on his arm to stop him for a second. "Hey, you good at writing or history?"

"Yeah."

"Tell him you were helping a friend with a paper. I have a history class I'm making up this summer, so if he asks, it's a paper on socialism in fiction."

"Thanks," he said. He reached for the door handle again and opened it this time.

"Hey, wait." I stopped him again. He looked at me. I don't know why I did it, but I did...I kissed him. We were just fucking around, and I knew that, but hooking up didn't mean I couldn't have the decency to kiss him goodnight. I wasn't a complete scumbag or something.

I'm not sure why our conversation kept getting under my skin, why I couldn't stop thinking about what he said on the drive home, but it got to me. Did he mean his dad was shitty about letting him have fun once in a while, or was he talking about something bigger? His dad wanting to fix him didn't imply anything good, and I was worried about him. But I couldn't find out more, not without calling him or something, texting, whatever. But it wasn't like I'd saved his number, so that wasn't an option anyway. I did know I was frustrated with myself. *No strings,* I reminded myself. The thing is, it didn't hurt me to recognize he was a human being with emotions and things that happened in his life outside of what we were doing, but I also knew getting attached would screw me over a little, if I started to see him as a friend. This wasn't friends with benefits, it was sex. And reminding myself of that was a good thing.

"Hey." Alex started talking to me the second I walked in the door. "That Tris kid has a giant dick, huh?"

"Shut up," I groaned, flopping on the couch beside him.

"Come on, you weren't quiet, man." That in itself was thoroughly embarrassing. I mean, I didn't usually bring hookups back anytime I thought a roommate might be around, but that was the first time I'd actually brought one back since living with Alex, and I guess I hadn't anticipated him calling me out on it as soon as I walked in the door. "It's cool. So how big was it?"

"I dunno," I grumbled. *Were we really talking about this?* I regretted sitting down on the couch instead of making a beeline to my room and avoiding this conversation altogether, but I had the feeling saying something wasn't exactly something I could avoid. Alex seemed dead set on talking about it.

"I bet I'm bigger."

Apparently, that's what the whole conversation was about. It was some sort of twisted measuring contest. I rolled my eyes and leaned as far to the other side of the couch as I could.

"You want to look and tell me? Or hell, maybe I can do what he did, and you can tell me what feels bigger, mine or his."

"Seriously? Are you actually saying the words I'm hearing from your mouth right now?"

"What, it isn't like he's your boyfriend or anything, is he? You sort of acted like he was just a hookup. You meet him on Grindr or something?"

"Creep," I said, trying to joke back. We should have played FIFA instead of talking. "I'm going to study." I could explain more another day, sometime when he wasn't pushing to get his own chance. Right then, I wasn't having it. What annoyed me is I probably would have been down any other time. Alex was a pain in the ass a lot of the time, but he was a good roommate, tidy and generally chill, and he was also pretty convenient dick. There's not a lot more convenient than someone willing to live with you but also fuck you when you needed or wanted it, no strings attached. It was basically my dream arrangement.

I didn't like strings. Strings got messy and tangled. Strings got you fucked over. But for some reason, I couldn't bring myself to sleep with him, not right then. So, I went to my room and I studied, and nothing happened between me and Alex that night. At least a lot happened between me and my socialism in fiction paper. That part of my conversation with Tristan wasn't a lie...I really did have a paper to write.

Tristan wasn't at the pool the next day when it opened. I didn't know where he was, but he wasn't there.

"You see Tristan anywhere?" James asked, which only made it more apparent he wasn't there. I wondered why he was asking too; if those two had somehow decided to do something, be something when I wasn't looking. Why else would James have wanted to know? I tried not to let the feelings of jealousy to the forefront of my brain. I wasn't jealous. I couldn't be. No strings.

"Nope," I said. "I wasn't looking for him." I was lying through my teeth about that one. I'd looked for him and failed to find him. I had to be honest with myself though: on my break, I really wanted to go into the office, get his number, and text him to see what was up. That seemed like a bad idea, especially if, by some strange twist of fate, he wasn't there because of me. Maybe he was avoiding me, I didn't know. I wasn't one to be self-conscious or have some sort of fragile ego or whatever else. The truth is, at the beginning of the summer, if Tristan had not shown up for the day, I probably would have been happier to not deal with him. But today, his absence felt like a problem, and I had to ask myself if it was because of me that he wasn't there, if somehow he didn't want to come to the pool, to face me, to listen to my authority there if he tried to do some stupid shit. You know, after he'd pounded the living daylights out of me in bed the night before and I'd told him again and again how great his cock was inside me.

"If you see him, let me know." The statement from James really threw me, made me more paranoid they were something I didn't realize.

"Why?"

"Because I wanted to talk to him. What's your issue with him anyway, that you're that annoyed over me talking to him?" he asked me, and then I really felt like I'd have to eat my words or something.

"I don't have an issue. I mean, if you want to talk to him, that's your prerogative." I was backed into a corner and basically giving my permission, not just my permission but encouragement, for James to go talk to him. Not like anyone needed my opinion, but I'd been so dismissive and against James getting to know him because Tristan was stupid before that. Part of me felt fiercely protective, though, very much not okay with James badgering him. Another part of me was concerned that it was obvious how I felt. As soon as the thought of *what if they talk and Tristan likes him?* hit my brain, I tried to push it out. There was no room for a thought like that in my life. So be it. If they got together, great. It was probably best for me if it did. So, I promised James I'd let him know if I saw Tristan, and when Tristan finally showed up three hours before the pool closed, I did exactly that.

"He's here," I told James coolly, trying not to let on that I gave a single fuck. Because I didn't give a single fuck. Why should I?

"Cool, thanks," he answered.

I hated the fact I sort of hoped, as stupid as he could be, that Tristan would wind up in my section. I tried to channel every part of me that was furious at him the first week or so of the pool being open, tried to pry that back to the surface of my brain, but even when I was thinking about his attention-seeking behavior, I was looking at James leaning over the edge, talking to him. I was wondering what they were saying to each other; if Tristan was into him or what they were discussing. I was—God forbid—really, really fucking jealous.

Shit.

I'd caught feelings.

I don't *do* feelings.

Chapter Eleven

"Hey, Connor." I looked down at the cool water and felt Tristan splash it on my feet.

"Hey." I didn't want to let on that this conversation had me feeling any kind of way. And the reality was, this conversation on its own didn't. It was simply the overall conversation and interactions with him that did me in, that felt overwhelming.

"What's up?"

"Working. Obviously," I said. "Why were you so late today?" As soon as I'd said the words, I wished with everything in the world that I could take them back, stuff them down my throat. The fact I'd noticed was annoying enough, but now he knew I noticed, and it was even worse. For all my fear of literal drowning, I seemed to be metaphorically drowning and there wasn't a damn thing I could do.

"I had to take care of some shit for my dad," he said and then he reached for my ankle, just like he'd done the first day to ask me my name. This time, he didn't need to do anything to get my attention—he already had it—so I wasn't sure what his angle was. But then his thumb grazed my skin softly, running along my foot as he fluttered his eyes up at me. I realized there wasn't an angle at all, and it hit me there was a part of him, however small, that just wanted to touch me. I smiled at him and then I felt stupid for doing it. Just because I had the smallest, barely there sort of feelings for him didn't mean I needed him to know they existed at all.

I still had time to squash my interest down, ignore it, fix it, make myself feel anything but what I was feeling before he knew at all that I was into what he was doing. I could still pretend this didn't exist, and I could save myself from the idea I might like him.

"I have to rotate stations," I said. "See you later." I cut myself off before I could say his name, call him Tris, the exact same nickname I'd used in bed. I didn't want to use any term of endearment, even a nickname. I wasn't in this. I couldn't afford to be.

So, I changed stations. At first, he didn't follow. Maybe it was like he knew I wasn't wanting him to. But then he did, he swam over to my section, and I could see him following me and James following him, and I wanted so badly to walk away, but once I was in my section, I couldn't. I was on duty. I couldn't walk away from him or anyone else. All I could do was pretend to not see him, pretend to look at anyone but him, and that helped until I needed to clean the bathrooms again.

Clearly, he'd seen me slip away because when I turned around, hands full of supplies, there he was. "You want to pretend the door is jammed again?" he asked, and lord knows I wanted to. I wanted to desperately.

"I can't," I said.

"No one will see." He was reassuring me, and I wanted to accept, to let him push me against the door and do anything he wanted to do to me. I could have let him, could have felt his hands on my chest as he pushed me toward the door, fucked me like I didn't have anywhere else to be, but the reality was letting myself do that was only getting me sucked in deeper. He stepped closer to me, put his hand on mine on the bucket. "I can make sure we stay quiet if you want."

"How?" I asked. I was playing with fire, letting myself get tempted. He put his free hand on my chin, drawing me closer, and kissed me. I kissed back because I wanted to, needed to, was dying for it, and I tugged at his lip with my teeth before kissing him again. I rested my forehead against his.

"That quiet enough?" I nodded, and he used the hand that was on my bucket to try to guide it down. The movement snapped me to my senses, reminded me I had to stay strong in this. I was going to get burned so bad if I let him move forward, do anything else.

"I can't do this."

"You can," he said. "We're alone in here."

"No, I mean...I can't. Any of this, like...at all." I didn't want to have this conversation in the first place, let alone here while I was at work and horny and desperate for him. I was so close to taking it back, to telling him never mind, forget it, I wanted this and wanted him. The truth was, I really, really did. One speck of resistance on his part, and I would have given up.

"Is this because, uh...is it because of the drowning thing?"

"No." It was, but it wasn't. I'd managed to finally mentally separate between the Tristan who faked a drowning and the Tristan who already had my attention, the one who I wanted desperately to cling to. In my mind, they were now different people. "I mean, I don't know. Maybe. It's about...it's about a lot of things." Letting him do what he wanted, letting him suck me off, all of that would have been easier than having this conversation, especially because most of me didn't want to talk about it at all.

"Is it about James?"

"Sort of." It wasn't even remotely about James. "You know he really likes you. I think if you wanted, you could probably hook up with him."

"You're seriously telling me to hook up with someone else? Really? That's...that's nice, Connor. Thanks." I could tell I'd upset him. But I was upsetting myself, too, and it would be a whole hell of a lot easier if he didn't see that telling him to look elsewhere was hurting me as much as it hurt him.

"You don't have to," I told him. "I was just saying you could if you were interested. He's clearly down."

"Got it. Thanks. Good luck with the toilets." He didn't sound angry over the rejection at all. Instead, he looked more like a kicked puppy.

He was gone before I could really say anything else to him, and I was thankful cleaning bathrooms was a task I did alone. I didn't want anyone else to see me right then, not when I was fucked up over this. I wanted to cry. Fuck, I *did* cry. I couldn't wrap my brain around why it mattered, why I cared so much, why I was into him. I focused on what he'd done, the bad things, the ways he'd tried to get my attention. I focused on how pissed off I'd been the first time I kissed him, how much I wanted to slap him then. No matter how hard I tried to make myself angry, I couldn't do it. It should have been easy enough. Drowning was a touchy topic for me, and it should have been the one thing that kept me angry at him forever, but I couldn't bring myself to get mad at him or to hate him or dislike him or anything. Instead, all I felt was sadness.

I wanted to say I was sorry and fix things. I wanted to apologize and tell him why I was so confused and messed up and try to get with him again. But I couldn't backtrack, not when I'd been strong enough to tell him to go away in the first place. I'd been strong and being weak now wasn't helping either of us. It wasn't. I was trying to convince myself of that.

I half-expected to see him talking to James when I got out of the bathrooms, but I didn't. James was there, but Tristan was nowhere to be found. "You see Tristan?" I asked James and then I hated myself for asking. It seemed obvious I actually cared, and that was not even remotely okay.

"Nope." He stayed tight-lipped, not talking to me, and I wondered for a second if Tristan had said something to him. "He disappeared before you went to clean the bathrooms, and I haven't seen him since." At least it was obvious the two of them hadn't talked, but the second I thought that, I got angry with myself. I wanted them to talk, to hook up, to do anything, right?

I would say I don't know what possessed me, but I knew exactly what possessed me. Before the end of the day, before I could go home, before the office was locked for the night, I flipped through the files, pulled out a phone, and tapped the number he'd given me for the paperwork into my own phone. I wasn't going to text or call him. I had promised myself that. But something about having his number made me feel better anyway. I was hopeless, maybe a little reckless and stupid, but for the rest of the night, I felt like shit and didn't want to talk. That's why, when I got home and heard Alex talk shit, say something like "no big-dicked Tris today? Shame. Need mine instead?" I flipped him off and went to my room, locked the door, and shamefully jacked off.

I say shamefully because as much as I tried to think of anything else, to watch porn, to focus on any dick but his, my brain was right there, trained on him, on how good he felt, how he made me feel, not just when he did what he was doing but also after, when his arms were around me, when his lips were on my neck and back and shoulder, when he was telling me how good I sound when I come. My brain fixated on that, and I hated thinking about what he said and did. I would've rather thought of nothing than of him, but he was the one I couldn't get my mind off. I did what I had to do. I got off, I threw up, and I took a long shower. I didn't text Tristan.

Chapter Twelve

I broke something inside myself when I told him no, but it sort of seemed like maybe I broke something in him, too, because for a week, he was gone. I think the way I moped was obvious, because Maria asked me what was wrong with me every single day, and every single day I said I was fine, that I didn't get why she kept asking me, because clearly I was all right. Which, honestly? Bullshit.

But work friends didn't need to know I wasn't doing well. And work friends weren't the only ones who had noticed how shitty my mood was. Alex wouldn't get off it, either, badgering me about it after work. "Damn, the big-dicked dude didn't come home with you again?" he asked. For all he knew, Tristan was only ever a hookup, a one-and-done situation, so I'm not sure why he wouldn't shut up about him. "Is that why you're in such a shitty mood? I gotta be honest, Connor, if you're missing one part of him specifically, it isn't like I don't have one." My first response was to roll my eyes and slink out of the room, frustrated and annoyed that another person had called me out on my attitude.

To be honest, though, Alex had a point. I didn't know Tristan well enough to miss all of him, so to me, it started to make sense it was his dick I missed most, given all the times I jerked off thinking about the time we'd fucked. So, I did what any rational human being would do in that situation. I grabbed the bottle of lube and a condom from my bedside table, walked back into the living room, and tossed it in Alex's lap. "You seriously offering? Because fuck it, let's go. I'm down." Alex looked at the lube and back up to me almost like he didn't believe he'd finally worn me down after weeks of hinting and then eventually flat-out asking.

"Seriously?" He was incredulous.

"What, you have something better to do?" I asked him.

"I can cancel my plans," he said, but we both knew he was bullshitting anyway. From there, it was a mad scramble, like he wanted to get himself undressed before I could change my mind. We didn't bother picking a room, his or mine, so we stayed on the couch instead and there wasn't any real lead-up to anything. He offered, I accepted, and then the next thing I knew I was riding him on the couch, one foot perched on each side of his legs as I sank onto him. I didn't really look at him much at all, my back to his chest as he held my waist and guided me down before holding me in place for a bit and thrusting hard and fast into me until it was nearly too much.

"Jesus," I groaned, and I think he took my statement as a request for him to slow down, because he did. But it wasn't a complaint, and the second I took over the pace, I aimed to go just as fast. This wasn't sex for lust or pleasure or anything else. This was sex for the sake of sex, for something to do, for a way to get my mind off other stupid things, or hell, because he'd offered so many times that turning him down again felt ridiculous at this point. It wasn't like I wasn't okay with hooking up with him, so I wasn't sure why I'd said no for so long.

The whole thing was rushed, but fast was okay. I don't think we ever even kissed or talked through it at all, mostly groaning and interjecting an expletive or two. Eye contact never happened either, and when I finished first, the last thing I wanted was for him to keep fucking me, so I crawled off him, got on my knees, rolled off the condom, and helped him out another way. I don't remember him asking me to, or me saying I wanted to, or anything else. It felt like a blur, but not in the good, blissful, oh-my-God-that-was-awesome kind of blur, but more of the "cool, we fucked, glad that happened" kind of blur where it was completely insignificant. It just...existed.

After, we didn't share any sort of intimate moment or connection or anything else. When I finished, I grabbed my shirt and cleaned myself off, grabbed my bottle of lube, and like the complete dumbass I am, I said "thanks," before walking to my room. We really didn't talk about what we did after that, not much, outside of him asking if I wanted to fuck again. The thing is, I really wasn't against the idea of doing it again, but the next time he asked, I was on my way to class and suggested we do it later. Then I completely forgot, and he never bothered asking another time.

The day after that, Tristan was back at the pool as if nothing had happened. He didn't make an effort to come to my section, but he also didn't avoid me completely. When he was in my section, he didn't do the thing where he grabbed my ankle. I figured I'd basically squashed whatever was there when he didn't do that. It was a pretty clear indicator he wasn't interested anymore, it seemed like. I felt guilty more than anything. He was a good guy, ridiculous attention-seeking flaws aside, and I cut him off without any warning after we'd had something good going. Then, I'd gone and gotten fucked by someone else for no reason other than I wasn't getting nailed by him.

That part of summer wasn't one of my prouder moments, and every time I looked at him, I'd think about how badly I'd fucked up all over again. I was hitting a real low there, and I felt like a complete asshole about it.

It looked a little bit like Tristan was getting cozy with James. There weren't any real signs of affection there at first, but when James would say hi to him, Tristan didn't blow him off or ignore him anymore. He said hi and then turned back to whatever he'd been doing, and that seemed like something. At least, that connection was more of something than I wanted to get in the middle of.

It was easier when he wasn't there. Before he came back, I could almost forget him, and over that two weeks, even if I couldn't fully forget the person, I could almost-not-quite forget the feelings I had for him. Yeah, the feelings I had convinced myself were just horniness. I could act like it had all been a one-off thing. But when he was there, it was really hard to see him, to try to catch his eye, and see him turn the other way. We'd somehow gone from me being completely, horribly, definitely uninterested in him, pretty much hating his guts, to us being the opposite: me trying for his attention, and him acting like I didn't exist. I was too old for this kind of thing, to be lusting helplessly after someone, so I did what I did best and pretended I couldn't care less. At least when I had tried to get his attention, it had been by a small wave and not by, say, faking a drowning. I'd say one of us had sense, but I couldn't be entirely sure that was true, either, and if it was true, it wasn't necessarily the one of us I wanted to believe it was.

Chapter Thirteen

After several days, I couldn't take the silence anymore. Him being near me, that close, and not talking to me was overwhelming. At first, I used the tactic I'd employed the first time I wanted his attention and stayed after work, hanging out by the drinking fountain. He came over, got a drink, and didn't say a word to me. I couldn't tell if he was making a point—that he was over what we did—or if it was his way of waiting for me to open the conversation instead. When he walked away, I felt like shit, wishing I'd said something and wondering why I didn't. I knew why I didn't, obviously, but I kicked myself for it anyway.

I should have taken his obvious indifference as the rejection it appeared to be, but apparently, I was really, really into tormenting myself. What else is new? The next day after work, for the first time all summer, I decided it was time to swim. I slipped into the water in the section of the pool he was in. It didn't take long, only a few minutes really, for him to swim closer. He looked at me, but he didn't talk. When James walked by, I panicked and slipped under the water, worried he'd see and assume there was something I wasn't telling him. There obviously wasn't, not after the way Tristan wasn't talking to me and had been gone for ages, not after everything I'd done, but I didn't need James's assumptions messing shit up even more.

When I went under the water, though, Tristan did too. He looked at me, got closer to me. I tried to convey every possible form of apology I could with my eyes, and I even said I was sorry, but that was only met with a bubbly "what?" on his part. So, I did the semi-logical thing and let myself up for air (I didn't need any real drownings that summer, especially not my own) and then went back down. Tristan did the same, and instead of letting my words speak for themselves, I swam forward and kissed him. At first, I was tentative, half-expecting he'd push me away. Instead, he pulled me closer and I let myself get into it, let myself kiss him like I meant it until my lungs burned and begged for oxygen, my tongue flicking across his chlorine-water-coated lips.

When I let go and came up for air, he stood up in the water and blinked at me, cocking his head to one side like he didn't know where I wanted him to go from there. But I wasn't sure either. I felt like a complete idiot. I was supposed to dislike him, was supposed to avoid him, should have been helping James get with him. He'd given every indication he was over it, too, but somehow, I'd ended up kissing him underwater like a lovesick child playing mermaids in the deep end.

So, I ran. Without a glance back, without a towel, without anything, I got out of the pool and walked quickly to my car. I sat down inside it and closed myself in.

And then I lost my shit. I groaned at myself and pounded the steering wheel and half-yelled. "Stupid, stupid, *stupid*, Connor, how could you be so fucking stupid?" My eyes burned and I tried to convince myself it was the pool water and not tears threatening to spill over as I screamed at myself for what I'd done. I slammed my hands on the hot steering wheel again. But then the car door opened, and Tristan sat down next to me completely uninvited. I didn't want to consider how much of my meltdown he might have witnessed. The last thing I needed was any idea of the fact he might have seen me losing my shit in the parking lot of the pool.

He didn't mention it at all, thank God. Instead, he put his hand on mine on the gearshift.

"Drive."

I didn't have to ask where or tell him what I was doing. We both knew. And when I got home, he barely waited, opening his door before I could even get mine open. After three and a half weeks of dancing around this, summer was halfway over, and we didn't have time to talk about it or second-guess what we were doing. It felt fast and ephemeral and overwhelming. I didn't want to think about it, either. I just wanted to do this and have this before it was too late, before there was no more summer left for whatever was happening between us.

As I went up the stairs, he wasn't shy, reaching out to pinch my ass. And when I was unlocking the door, he got bolder, holding my waist and kissing my neck. "Is this okay?" he asked, and I reached around to pull him closer, let him nuzzle my neck more than he'd been doing.

"Yeah," I told him, and he stayed that close as we went inside. He leaned back against the front door when it was closed, pulling me toward him. His fingers were entwined with mine and I kissed him, feeling the flutter of his breath on my lips and the way he held me tightly. "I fucked up," I told him. I meant I'd fucked up about a lot of things: telling him I couldn't do this with him, sleeping with Alex when I was only thinking about him all the time, all of it. I didn't go into details, though. I couldn't. "Are you mad at me?" Way to sound like an overemotional shithead.

"I was waiting for you to come to me. You said you couldn't do this, so I figured if you changed your mind, you'd let me know," he told me. "I gave you a chance, over by the drinking fountain?" I'd been so stupid. He *had* waited for me to say something and I hadn't, instead taking his silence for the rejection it wasn't like a complete dumbass.

"I changed my mind," I said, and his lips were on mine again, hands on my waist as he walked me toward my room.

"I noticed."

From there, he wasted no time in getting me stripped out of my lifeguard trunks, tossing them on the ground and kissing me. He lifted my legs, folding me like a cheap card table, and spread them apart enough to kiss me between them. He kissed up my thigh, taking his sweet time. His breath was warm and focused, and as he got closer to where he was going, he bit my ass, probably hard enough to leave a mark. My writhing on the sheets didn't stop him, and it shouldn't have. I wasn't looking for him to stop. He needed to keep going. I needed him to. I was getting harder and whimpering, but all my need was from how good it felt. His tongue was warm on my skin, especially in the most intimate parts of me, and without the mad rush of the first time we'd done this, feeling how careful and gentle he could be drove me crazy. He was kneeling on the bed and my knees were somewhere near my ears or something, I don't know. Sometimes the details get fuzzy and I wonder how he managed flexibility from me I didn't know was possible. But the thing is, I'd contort myself in a whole hell of a lot of ways for a guy to eat my ass like that, so it makes sense in hindsight, I think.

"Fuck me," I said, reaching down to pull him up my body. I figured it would be enough to spur him along, but as he pulled back, he smiled at me.

"You're going to ignore me forever and then expect I'm just gonna fuck you right away?" I'd never met someone so willing to take charge and push like that. I was used to having some sort of say, some sort of...control, I guess. Goes to show how much of a control freak I could be about some things. But Tristan wasn't interested in that. Right then, he was interested in taking his time. He kissed down my leg again, unfolding me and placing a kiss on the sole of my foot. He laid his body over mine and bit my lip, tugging at it. "You really want me to fuck you now?"

"Yeah," I said. He always threw me off guard, left me feeling a little breathless, and I swear that kind of thing both frustrated and intrigued me about him. It had frustrated me from the beginning, from the very first day when he'd splash me or tug at my lanyard. He took charge in a lot of ways, and that terrified me. So when I answered yes, I hoped I'd get it and I figured I wouldn't, but Tristan never really stopped surprising me, and in the spirit of that surprise, this time he gave me exactly what I asked for.

For every way he could be an immature brat in public, he was different when we were alone. He told me how beautiful I was, how good I looked with the light streaming in through the window and falling on my skin, tanned from hours on the lifeguard stand. It was damn near reverent and I didn't understand how someone could really think all that about me. I mean, yeah, I'm not hideous, but he was talking me up like some sort of hype man, telling me I was amazing and gorgeous.

"God, every inch of you is perfection," he told me. "You're so stunning, holy crap." He kissed my abs, bit them a little, told me how sexy I was. All the talk was overwhelming, the way he poured kindness over me, praised me for who I was as a person. It was hard not to get sucked into believing it was true, that I was worthy of someone taking their time like this. But in that moment, I *did* believe him. I hung on his every word and it left me with a little less than complete and utter self-loathing for a change. He reached past me to the side table. "Connor?"

"Yeah?"

"You're out of condoms."

Fuck. Was I? I hadn't done that much that summer, but I rolled over on my side to look. Clearly, I hadn't been optimistic, having purchased a three-pack. "Are you clean?"

Tristan snorted. "I can just suck you off." I guess my groan made it clear I wanted more, because he pulled out his phone, tapped at it, and handed it over. "Test results. We good now?" He kissed my neck again.

"I hooked up with someone." If he was willing to prove he was clean, and I couldn't, this didn't seem fair. I sighed again.

"Ask your roommate." I started, thinking maybe he knew we hooked up and I should ask Alex if he was clean, since he was the only other person I'd been with lately. "Surely, he has condoms." Oh. I scrambled and tugged on shorts, but when Alex's room was empty, I ended up grabbing two and scribbling an IOU on a sticky note on his desk. I wasn't waiting around for permission. Forgiveness was easier, and I needed Tristan inside me.

His lips were on my collarbone as he entered me, and he held my hand when he pushed deeper. I wanted to cry.

I'd brushed him off as annoying, as too young to know better about anything, hell, I'd brushed him off for being almost too good even more recently than that, and here he was, ignoring all of that (if he'd ever even realized I'd had those issues in the first place). He was genuinely making it hard for me not to hate myself for being completely wrong, while also making me want to like myself as much as he seemed to. The things he made me feel were confusing. It was overwhelming. But it was also amazing.

He draped his body over mine again, my legs together as he turned me on my side. When he gripped my thigh, he laid down on me, pushing into me and nosing at my jaw.

"You're so sexy, Connor, God, you're sexy." He was talking enough for both of us, so I didn't say much. I whimpered, I moaned, I writhed, but he talked, telling me he liked how I felt. "You're really tight," he told me, and I crumbled under the kisses he left on my shoulder. He pulled out of me and moved me, "roll over," and then he was inside me again. He enveloped me, lying on my back, holding me close and pulling me toward him. If I didn't already feel overwhelmed by the intensity, this would have done me in, but this position felt like the natural extension of how he was taking me, how he was giving me all he had. I reached behind my head to draw him in for a kiss, and he took his time, exploring me with the hand he wasn't using to support himself as he deepened the kiss.

"Fuck, Tris..." I groaned, but my thoughts weren't really coherent. They're still not coherent when I think about it, the way he made me feel then. "You feel so good." I wanted to say something better, something more, something on par with the way he'd lavished praise on me, but I couldn't. He deserved that, and I couldn't give it to him, because he'd fried my brain. Words didn't work for me right then. He'd said so many incredible things about me, but in that moment, all my thoughts were frozen. It was just me, him, the feeling of him in me. He touched me, stroked me, took me until I was making a damn mess of the bedding I was on, and then he was coming too.

"Come here," he told me, and I did. I let him have anything he wanted, let him guide me any way he wanted. "It's going to be okay. Tell me how to make it okay." He kissed me and used his thumb to wipe a tear from my face. I didn't even know I was crying.

Chapter Fourteen

I didn't mean to cry. For a few minutes, I didn't even know *why* I was crying, but as he wrapped his arms around me, asked me what was wrong, it became impossible not to practically overshare. "I'm so sorry," I said, choking my words through strangled sobs into his shoulder.

"What are you sorry for? You don't need to be sorry." He told me that, but it was hard for me to believe he didn't know why I should be apologizing. I had so many reasons to be sorry, if I was honest with him, with myself.

"I hated you." It probably wasn't fair to him to be so blunt, to tell him flat-out how I felt at first, but I felt like I should be open about it, just in case now was when he'd want to dip, want to leave and forget this. If he didn't know, that would be good enough reason to end this, whatever it was. I couldn't exactly call it no strings attached anymore. There were definite strings.

"Oh. I knew that," he told me, kissing my nose. "You had good reasons to hate me. I pretended to drown." He ran his fingertips up and down my spine as I laid my head on his chest. "I wanted your attention, but you know...I'm stupid sometimes when I'm horny." I resisted the urge to laugh at that despite my tears and frustration.

"It wasn't because of that," I told him, but I realized quickly that was a lie. It was at least in part because of that. "You know I made somebody drown once?" If anything was a dealbreaker for someone, it was probably going to be that. For a solid decade, I'd had nightmares about it, too, about his blue-tinged lips and the glassy look in his eyes, the sound of splashing and panic. It haunted me, especially knowing the guy's drowning was all my fault.

"Jesus, Connor, are you serious?" He backed away from me, but only by about an inch. He kept his arms around me, too, but his hand on my back stilled and he pressed it flat instead of rubbing. He wasn't scared away by the statement, apparently, but he did seem startled by it. I get it. My confession was a bit much to throw at someone post-sex. Well, anytime, actually...

"I made someone drown" is sort of a lot no matter what activity you'd just been engaged in. I'd imagine it would have been just as bad any other time too.

"I was eight," I told him. "He was drowning, and I tried to get the lifeguard's attention, but he didn't hear me yelling. I think maybe he thought we were just fucking around. I tried to pull the kid out myself, but I couldn't."

"Yeah, but none of that makes it sound like you did anything wrong. It sounds like you tried to *help* him," he told me.

"I did! It was my fault though," I answered, praying he'd understand.

"How was it your fault? Did you hold him under the water too long or something?" He furrowed his brow.

"He was playing with his friends," I told him. "I didn't know him or anything, not really. But he was playing, and I was screwing around, doing handstands and stuff, kinda showing off. I kicked him in the head. And then he didn't come up again."

"That's not your fault, honey," he said, pulling me closer and hooking one of his legs around my leg. He brushed my hair away from my forehead. "It was an accident. And then you tried to help him. You did everything you could."

"I kicked him. I didn't mean to, but I did it, and then he drowned. That's on me. All of that's on me. If I wouldn't have kicked him, he'd probably still be alive," I cried, choking on my tears and sucking in a breath. He soothed me and tried to calm me down, holding me close.

"So that's why you were mad at me? That's...God. I kept fucking around, and you kept trying to get me to stop and instead of doing what you told me to, oh gosh..." He closed his eyes. "I'm so sorry. I'm *so* sorry." I had been really angry with him, held such a grudge against him. Hell, I'd thought anyone even remotely interested in him was an idiot.

"I thought you were going to die," I told him honestly. "And I thought it was going to be my fault, that I didn't watch you enough or make sure you were careful when you had been so wild. I was so scared." I was only crying harder now, and he was apologizing again and again, but I wasn't angry with him. "It's not your fault," I told him. "You had no clue. But it scared me, you scared me so badly."

"I know. I'm so sorry. I'm...I swear if I could go back, I never would have done any of that."

I nodded and swallowed heavily.

"It's a wonder you even set foot in a pool," he told me.

"My mom thought if I learned to swim, the nightmares would stop, so she pushed me into taking more swimming lessons. Then I got really good at it, and I thought if I got better, I could stop myself from drowning. And even though I hate lifeguarding, sometimes it's nice to know maybe I could make up for fucking up and not saving him."

"You couldn't have saved him," he told me. "You have to stop blaming yourself for it. You couldn't have saved him, sweetie. You couldn't." I'm not really sure when he'd progressed from sex to pet names, but it was probably somewhere between cuddling and the intensity of the confessions I was sharing with him. The thing is, I didn't mind it at all. The progression felt natural, like it was supposed to happen, supposed to be like that. And he was trying to make me feel okay. I don't think anything he said right then would have made me believe it wasn't my fault, but he was trying, and for that I was grateful. "It makes sense why you were so mad at me. I mean, obviously it did before. What I did was shitty, no matter how you spin it. But I get it now." He sighed softly and I desperately wanted him to stop apologizing to me. I didn't want to talk about the past anymore.

"I thought you hated me," I said. I was trying to change the subject.

"Because I was being a dumbass? I didn't hate you for stopping me. I liked any attention I got from you, honestly. I feel bad for that now, but...but it's true," he said.

"No, I mean in the supply room when I freaked out and said we couldn't, you know...I don't know. And then you were gone." He cracked a smile then and part of me felt offended he found it funny, but then he put his hand on my cheek.

"You really thought that was about you?" he asked. Him saying that made me feel stupid for thinking his absence was about me, like I was some sort of narcissist or something for thinking it might be about me at all.

"It was just the timing, is all," I tried to say, tried to deflect a little bit, make it seem like anyone should have drawn the same conclusion. In all honesty, it wasn't an outlandish conclusion to draw. He was gone right after I yelled at him, and me thinking he'd left intentionally made sense.

"I didn't hate you. I don't hate you. It wasn't about that, but I think the space probably did us both some good to make sure, you know? Unless you're planning on freaking out on me again."

"I'm not," I said.

"Good. For what it's worth, I did miss you a lot," he said. Before I could say anything back or ask for any details about why he was gone, he kissed my forehead. "You hungry?"

Chapter Fifteen

"Holy crap, Connor. It's so girthy. How do you even get your mouth around that?" He half whispered it, half laughed as he said it. "Gosh, you're really kinky if you can take something that big. I think I'm gonna need a second dick or something."

I was chewing so I couldn't respond right away, but I considered kicking him under the table for being so ridiculous in public. Once I could shift my bite of my burrito to my cheek, I was able to respond. "Oh my God, Tris, we're in public. You can't just say shit like that." I almost choked on the burrito from laughter, and it was better I didn't because he probably would have had a comment for that too. He would joke about something so immature and nonsensical, and I realized I wasn't as old and mature as I wanted to think I was, because I found that, and him, to be hilarious.

Interacting with him at the burrito place felt good. There wasn't pressure for it to be about secrets, like it was at work, or about sex, like it was at my place. At the local joint, which was practically a shack given the ramshackle way it was assembled, it was different. In those ratty, threadbare booths, we could talk. It also felt like it didn't have to be as deep or dark of a conversation as we'd had earlier in my bedroom. Everything felt lighter and freer.

And, of course, it also didn't suck that he could crack dick jokes about burritos if we were going and getting those for dinner. For this to be the worst summer of my life, it was shaping up to not be entirely shitty, provided I could keep talking to him, so I did. For an hour, it was just that: dick jokes and burritos and me trying to lean across the table and steal kisses as quickly as he stole chips from my basket. It was almost cute. I wasn't used to bringing that much attention to myself, having some sort of weird PDA going on, but I didn't entirely mind.

"So you thought I was mad at you?" he asked, and I wondered why we were doing this here, in the middle of a burrito place, instead of someplace we could properly talk about it, where I didn't feel so self-conscious. A public display of affection felt far easier than an actual discussion about my feelings. So, I did what I thought I should do: gave a non-committal shrug and hoped my lack of actual answer answered his question enough to move on. "I wasn't mad at you, Connor. Just so you know."

"I told you to go fuck with James or whatever instead of me, then I came out of the bathrooms and you were gone," I said. "Then you stayed gone. For like a week, even. So yeah, I mean, maybe you weren't mad at me, but like I said earlier, the timing seemed a little...I don't know, specific?" I half mumbled the words and failed to fully meet his eyes. The last thing I wanted was to talk about this. It didn't matter. This wasn't anything, so I'm not even sure why I cared so much whether he hated me or not. Hell, maybe the sex would have been even hotter if he *did* hate me. But he insisted he didn't, and I felt weird even talking about it.

"Do you want to know why I was gone?" he asked, as if he was starting to get the message this wasn't my idea of a good conversation to have. He was giving me the option for us to not talk about this at all.

I shrugged again but then I felt bad because clearly, he was genuinely trying to tell me, so I nodded. "Yeah." I did kind of want to know.

"Oh, babe," he said, carrying on with the same pet names from the bedroom, "when I got there that day, I'd just gotten kicked out of my house. My dad went off on me and told me to get out. I figured I'd get my mind off of shit with you, but you said no, and then the friend I was crashing with decided to leave anyway. I was just catching a ride to his place. That's all me leaving was...remarkably shitty timing."

I couldn't imagine being so casual about something as jarring as getting kicked out of the house I lived in, but he said it as normally as if he'd told me he needed to get lunch or had a bad case of the hiccups. I was confused as hell. "Wait, you got kicked out?" I asked, and I placed my burrito back down because the whole thing was a lot to take in and I didn't have the capacity to both eat a burrito and hear his story at the same time. "Jeez. I'm sorry, Tris, wow, I...are you okay?"

"I'm fine. Just couch surfing at the moment. He has his own issues to deal with." This wasn't the first time Tristan had said something about his dad being unaccepting, having issues with who he was.

"I can't imagine trying to live with someone so homophobic," I confessed to him. "I'm sorry."

"Homophobic?" His face twisted, confused over what I'd said. "My dad's not homophobic, Connor." It felt like he was barely holding in laughter.

"You said he couldn't accept who you were!"

"Hey, no...he has a lot of issues, okay? But he's not homophobic or anything like that. He's, uh...he's not my real dad. My mom sort of got around a little bit, and I was lucky because he kind of always accepted me anyway, even though I'm not his kid. He really loved her, you know? But then she died, and he got stuck with me. He's always been super cool about it, letting me stay there and stuff even though I'm an adult now legally or whatever. Sometimes, you know, he just...he gets kind of annoyed and drunk, and then he tells me to get the fuck out. He'll get over it. It's okay."

It sounded like he needed rehab or an intervention or something. Getting drunk enough to kick out a kid he'd raised his whole life? That was a lot to take in. "Jesus," I sighed. "You're okay though?"

"I'm good. It's all okay. You going to eat the rest of that?" He nodded at my basket, at the half-eaten burrito there, and I was still hungry but another part of me didn't want to eat it in case I'd be getting laid again later. Burritos weren't exactly bottoming-friendly if you know what I mean.

"Eat it," I said, pushing my basket toward him and picking at the chips I'd left behind. For all I knew, he hadn't had a good meal lately, if he wasn't going home at night. "You have a place to stay tonight?"

Chapter Sixteen

Sex with Tristan was always an experience. We didn't fuck like I fucked other people, if that makes sense. It wasn't that he didn't seem to want to, or that I didn't let us do it that way, or whatever else. Tristan just seemed to have a preference, and it was one I liked a lot. Almost every time, he'd drape himself over me, cover me with his body, wrap his arms around me. I rarely rode him, and if I did, it was practically like riding someone through a bear hug, his arms looped over my shoulders or around my waist, and I liked it. When he held me, I felt safe. And warm. Really, really warm.

We had several opportunities to find out that night, and over the next couple of days. We'd fuck. We'd fall asleep. He'd wake me up by sucking me off "as thanks for letting me stay, Connor...seriously, have I told you how much I appreciate it yet?"

It was the best kind of way to wake up, to open my eyes to the warmth of his mouth around me, to let my fingers tangle in his hair as he got me off. Then, he'd ride with me to school. While I was in class, he'd sit outside and hang out, reading, talking to students he encountered, whatever, and then after my classes he'd hop back in the car. He knew how much I didn't want to get caught with him in case I was fired—we weren't supposed to hit on patrons, and it was highly unlikely that anyone would mistake it as friendship if they caught the way I couldn't take my eyes off him—so he always offered to hop out of the car a few blocks from the pool and walk the rest of the way. Tristan was a great guy like that.

Being around him so much was a lot, and every bit of it was wonderful. For days on end, I was with him constantly, except when I was on duty, and even then, he was right there, ever-present in whatever section I was in, like always. But then Alex got sick of hearing us at night, and he got tired of having someone else in the apartment all the time. After four days, we got the ultimatum. Unless Tristan was going to pay a third of the rent, he had to go. Alex had jokingly offered up the suggestion that Tris pay him "in other ways, if you know what I mean," but I shot that down before it ever got to Tristan's ears. Alex was a decent roommate, but he could be a real scumbag when he was horny. Instead, Tristan moved on to another couch, which left me sorely missing the way he had been waking me up and wearing me out.

On my lunch break, I needed him, wanted to feel him again, so I skipped eating and gave Tristan a look, a silent plea to meet me in the bathroom. "Missed me, huh?" he asked me, tugging me close and kissing me before he got on his knees. "Don't worry, I'll make it a good break for you." He ran his tongue slowly along my length and met my eyes. "How are you this sexy? Getting fucked at work? That's so hot."

Anytime he talked to me like that, it only got me harder, but then he got quiet to make sure no one found us. We had to be careful—the last thing either of us needed was to get caught like that. "Quiet," he whispered when he heard me start to get louder, my breath ragged as I rested my hand on his shoulder, cupped his chin to get him to look at me.

"I'm trying," I said softly. "You're too good at this for either of our own good." He smiled and went back to what he was doing, taking me deep and choking a bit as he did, pulling off me to kiss my hip bone as he used his hands to take over.

"You're so big. It's hard to take sometimes," he said. He was flattering me, knowing he was bigger, but I'd take it. I'd take whatever I could get. Neither of us were good at the whole no talking thing—we both liked to pepper our sex with words of encouragement and praise. Thankfully, he was skilled, good at making me feel good, and I was coming fast before I had to get back to work. I had enough time left on my lunch break to reciprocate, but he kissed me deeply, let me taste myself on his tongue as he ran his fingers along the nape of my neck. "Later," he said. "I don't want to risk it here." He was right in that we'd risked enough doing anything at work in the first place, but I appreciated that he didn't demand I try to make it even right away.

I didn't really think we'd been suspicious at all, but James eyed me after my lunch break. "You're in a good mood lately."

"Yup," I said. I figured the simpler my answer was, the less chance I had at giving away more information than I needed to. The more I spoke, the more I risked letting on that I was getting laid, and if I did, then I was risking letting on exactly who I was hooking up with, so I kept my mouth shut with the bare minimum. Unfortunately, James wasn't taking that as an answer. He had to keep going.

"You ever notice that Tristan always seems to be where you are?" he asked me.

"What do you mean?" I should have shut him down and said no, said it was a coincidence, said anything instead of asking a question. But honestly, I wanted to know what he was talking about, to know what he knew. Knowledge felt like power.

"You haven't noticed? He shows up around the time you get here and leaves around when you get off work. I can never seem to find him when you're on break either. It's almost like he is here with you or here for you or something," he said, trailing off a little bit.

"I guess I haven't been paying attention." I shrugged. "I haven't really noticed." I was lying through my teeth, but in fairness, he was never missing from me. I always knew exactly where he was.

"I'm just saying if I didn't know any better, I'd say you either have a stalker or an admirer or you two are fucking," James said, forcing a laugh, but his jealousy was palpable.

"You know what I think of him, so at the very least, that last part is a goddamn joke," I told him. It was hard even saying it. I had to let James believe I still hated Tristan with every fiber of my being. I hated lying but it felt necessary.

"I know, I know. I'm just saying, you really don't see how he tries to get your attention?"

I scanned the pool and looked for him, eyes landing on his lithe body, water running down his chest as he ran toward the end of the board, diving effortlessly. God, I desperately wanted to lick those droplets from his tanned skin. His body cut through the water like a knife through butter, and I wondered how I'd gone so long without noticing how perfect he was, how it had taken me feeling his body against mine to fully grasp the reality. I hadn't noticed before, because I hadn't let myself believe it was an option to notice him.

"Are you kidding?" I asked James, nodding toward him. "He seems pretty focused on his dives right now. That's him, right?"

"Of course, that's him. You smack your head after the whole CPR thing?" He rolled his eyes and I worried I'd played it too cool.

"It's been a long summer, man," I said. "Anyway, you taking trash out, or am I? Greg is going to kill us if it overflows any more than it is."

"I've got it." James sighed. It wasn't like I was actively trying to anger him or annoy him, but what was I supposed to say? That I was banging Tristan behind his back and keeping it quiet because I knew he was into him, and I didn't want to lose my job? Wasn't happening. As soon as James walked away, headed toward the trash cans, Tristan turned and looked at me. *Perfect timing*, I thought, because the smile he flashed was a winner. He scanned my body up and down with his eyes, biting his lip. It was more than a smile. It was a good, old-fashioned eye-fuck, and it was obvious that the second I was off work, if I wanted it to be, it was on. And damn, I really wanted it to be. James never had to know.

Chapter Seventeen

The afterglow did me in. Don't get me wrong, the sex itself was amazing every time with Tristan. But it was after, when he'd lay beside me and run his fingers along my arms, my chest, when the sunlight would filter in through the car window as I silently thanked myself for getting a car with seats that folded down flat to give us room for anything we wanted to do, that was the best part of all of it. He would kiss my shoulder and ask me how I was. "You okay?" he'd always say, and I'd nod and kiss him. Our hookups were the new normal for my summer, less sporadic and more intentional and consistent.

It was in the golden moments then, when it was a sweat-slicked early summer evening, the smell of sex in the car or the bedroom or that one time we fucked in his friend's shower in an otherwise empty apartment, that we talked. One time he asked me "So why'd you pick this college?"

"They've got the best nursing program in a four-state radius. I feel like I always knew I'd go here if I got accepted, and I did," I explained. I had always planned to go to this particular school, back when I was a high school freshman with a pamphlet hung in my locker. I leaped on applying as soon as I had the opportunity. I was shocked that I didn't even get waitlisted. The town itself wasn't even remotely a factor in my decision. It could have been an even worse shithole than I thought Springdale was, and I still would have done it for that school. "Are you excited about school?" I asked him.

"No," he admitted to me. "I'll do it though." I knew from that conversation that the nearest community college had never been his first choice. Tristan had even been accepted other places, better places. Places he actually *wanted* to go, places that would foster his talents. But after losing his mom, he lost so much of his will to put himself out there. Sure, he was bold with me, but apparently that was to mask his deep-seated insecurities and fears. He gave up on the desire to do anything more for himself than go to this school, get an entry-level job in his hometown, and stay put there forever. He worried if he left, the only dad he ever knew would never let him come home, and since he was sure his dad was about ready to let him move back in, he didn't want that. I hated seeing him settle. Community college wasn't a *bad* choice, necessarily. I just knew community college wasn't what he wanted, not at all tailored to his goals, and I felt like he deserved more. Tristan was a really bright guy with an amazing future ahead of him, and in my mind, he was giving up a lot of himself considering he had goals and dreams and places he wanted to be with focused programs for what he wanted to study. Our local community college didn't even offer pre-engineering kind of classes.

Tristan was the perfect mix of being stunningly gorgeous, but also artistically talented and mathematically minded. I didn't know anyone else who, given the opportunity to do anything in the world, would have chosen to double-major in visual arts and civil engineering. He wanted to sculpt and paint and sketch. He wanted to build buildings and bridges and waterways. He would have been brilliant at both, and instead he was sitting there, deciding to go to community college for a general studies associate's degree so he could end up substitute teaching an art class or whatever else that piece of paper could get him. Maybe I was a snob, and none of those careers were bad. And I had nothing against community college either. I'd gotten my EMR certification at one. It simply wasn't the right fit for *him,* and the things he wanted to get out of life. He was doing what would keep him close to home, and that was good but also terrible.

Part of me was hesitant to encourage him toward the school he really wanted. After all, if he stayed, we could keep doing this. We'd be in the same town, the same space, and this didn't have to end. If I pushed him to go, and he did, this would stop. Not that what we had *was* anything. It was never supposed to be anything, and we never really pushed to make our connection anything. It just existed for what it was, in a bubble, an ephemeral summer fling. But something in me wanted it to last, wished we could hold onto the moment and bottle it up and keep it safe. Every time I encouraged him to go, to pick one of his dream colleges, the chances of this lasting as anything but what it was grew less likely. But each time, he refused. He kept telling me he was happy with the choices he was making, and none of what I said about school mattered anyway. Tristan was the sort of guy who would find a way to be successful, likeable, amazing, no matter where he went or what he did.

When we were dressed again, we drove to a gas station, spent an hour in the parking lot drinking Slurpees. We exchanged kisses with bright-blue tongues, lazy and quiet under the glow of gas station lights. Only in hindsight does it occur to me that this mattered a lot for something that didn't matter at all. I feel like most people can pinpoint the relationships in their life that were significant: their first love, the first guy they move in with, the one they eventually marry, whatever. But the significance of this one was different. It was significant for its insignificance, for the fact it was never really...anything at all. What we had mattered in a lot of ways because it didn't. Matter, I mean.

This wasn't some big, grand relationship. What Tristan and I had together wasn't even a relationship at all. It was a moment in time, and it was absolutely ridiculous. We held hands and looked up through the sunroof of my car at what should have been stars, but they were blocked by the city lights. He listened to me whine about class and about my paper, which he offered to edit. English and History were his strong suits. To be fair, with his engineering goals, it seemed almost every subject was his strong suit. Those subjects weren't my best ones. But mostly, outside of that, we fucked.

I felt like we understood each other, and I spent a lot of time wishing I'd given him a chance from the beginning. It took us time to break down the walls I'd built, the ones where I was angry at him for trying to get my attention (and how he'd gone about that), but also the ones inside myself. They were walls of self-exile, of thoughts that I didn't deserve this affection or interest. Before Tristan, I'd had sex. I'd had a few short relationships. But with Tristan, things were different. The lack of pressure was a big part of the beauty of what we had, but the reality was, by the time I'd let myself embrace how I felt about him, summer was more than halfway over and we were desperately running out of time.

"I want to draw you," he told me one time. "Would you let me?"

I nodded, told him I would. He picked my bathroom of all places, had me strip down and turn on the shower. We piled towels onto the floor since the open shower curtain left the water puddling onto it. We didn't need the downstairs neighbors complaining of a leak, and if I had to do extra laundry to prevent that, I would.

"I'll be quick," he promised, kissing me, and then cranking the heat up, letting steam fill the room. It was an odd feeling, him being fully clothed and me being so exposed. He directed my every move, but then, when didn't he when we were in bed, guiding me with soft touches and kisses? It made sense. My hand was raised above me, flat against the wall, and I leaned into it. I let the water flow over me, in my hair, streaming down my arm, down my body, dripping off my nose and it tickled so much. I wasn't hard, obviously, even though I twitched at the thought of being so bare to him.

As he drew me, I stood as still as I could, not even wiping at the water that dripped down my face. He studied me, and out of the corner of my eye, face half-turned toward him but not enough so I could get a good look, I could watch the curve of a smile as he dragged his pencil along the page. He'd tilt his head to one side and his tongue would poke out between his lips as he focused intently. His brow would furrow as he'd bring the page a little closer to him, try to make sure the detail work was just right. "You have a great ass," he quipped.

"You tell that to all of your live models?" I asked him, resisting the urge to smile for what was supposed to be a serious portrait of me.

"Only the ones I really, *really* want to fuck later," he told me. "Just you, really." The words pooled in my stomach the way water pooled around my feet, the drain a little clogged from whatever—probably come, honestly. He made me feel worth looking at, worth admiring. I'd never felt like that before. "God, this is good."

"You're cocky," I told him. I was sure it wasn't an unwarranted assurance, because I had no doubt that he was talented, but I couldn't resist calling him out anyway.

"No. You're gorgeous, and that makes it good."

"You're gorgeous, and I'm not sure the stick figure I'd draw would do a good job of expressing that," I told him. "Art takes talent. If the picture's gorgeous, you've got a whole hell of a lot of it. It's not me."

When he was done, he told me to come take a look, and I turned the water off and drew the last dry towel around me as I stepped out and looked over his shoulder. "Damn, Tris. You could make a dumpster look like fine art."

"Come here, dumpster," he said, reaching over his shoulder to pull me down for a kiss. "You don't give yourself enough credit." He spoke the words against my lips, and it made my heart ache.

I wanted to cry. We had four weeks left, and then it was going to be goodbye, because after seeing that drawing, I'd be damned if he went to school in this town.

Chapter Eighteen

Where Tristan went to school wasn't at the forefront of my mind in the days after he drew me though. Not in the dying weeks of summertime, when I was more focused on how good it felt to have him in me, on me, around me. And that was what I was thinking about when he cornered me in the supply room once again. "Jesus, Tristan, you scared the shit out of me." I hadn't heard him come in, and I had to catch my breath for a second over how he'd startled me. I'd gotten more than my fair share of blowjobs in the supply room, but that particular day, he obviously he had more in mind than simply sucking me off.

He tugged me around a shelving unit and got his teeth on my earlobe. "You think anyone will notice if I fuck your brains out right here?" he whispered. His voice was gravelly and lustful in a way I didn't usually hear it. "You think you could stay quiet enough for me to do that?" I didn't know what had gotten into him, but I liked it, and I liked what he was suggesting.

"I have to clean toilets," I said. It was a weak protest at best. His hand in the front of my trunks worked to wear down my resolve quickly, and his lips moved to my neck to help with that too. I couldn't resist him, and he knew it, knew how to get at all my weaknesses.

"Give me ten minutes?" he asked. Ten minutes seemed reasonable. Ten minutes could be explained away by a clog I needed to fix before I could scrub.

"What's with you today?" I asked him, and he kissed me. He seemed ravenous and needy.

"Short summer," he told me. "Have to take you every chance I can get you, and I won't be able to come over later today." I nodded, turning and letting myself lean against the shelf in front of me. We were out of sight of the door, and provided I could be quiet, no one would notice us, I figured. He slid my trunks to my ankles and I'm not sure if he'd stashed it in the closet ahead of time or if he'd brought it with him, but his hand was slick with lube as he pushed his fingers into me. We didn't have time for him to go slowly, so he worked fast, rolling the condom on right after. When he was in me, it was a frenzied pace, and as much as I tried not to make a sound, the slap of his skin against mine with every thrust was more than enough to give us away had anyone walked in the room. But as he did that, no one did, or even tried. My eyes stayed locked on the door—I could see it through the shelving, and it was impossible not to think about how easily we could get caught, even if we quieted down were the door to open. And to be honest, I think that only made things hotter, harder, more intense because of the inherent risk, the idea I could lose my job, that he could get kicked out, that this was so uncalled for and so not okay for us to do.

The sex was hot and quick and every time I'd make a noise, he'd remind me someone might hear. That only made me want more. "God, yeah, Tris, just like that, fuck me harder," I pleaded quietly, voice squeaking as I tried not to make too much noise, and he did, going as fast and hard as he could. "I'm so close," I said, spilling onto the shelf in front of me. I'd clean it up later, I figured, but first all I could focus on was how he rubbed his thumb over my oversensitive tip as he kept pounding into me, biting into my shoulder a little as he came.

He was still inside me when light flooded the dark room, and it went back to pitch-black as soon as the door closed. We couldn't see who had entered, our eyes not adjusting quite yet to the changes in light in such a short amount of time. "Connor, you in here?" The voice horrified me. James. "Oh my God, holy shit. Oh my God." If there were any doubt that he'd seen us, it was removed with those words. My body was still draped over the shelves and Tristan hadn't gotten off me, out of me fast enough. We were both fully exposed.

"It's not what it looks like," I said, but it was exactly what it looked like and all three of us knew it. James had just seen the person he was interested in, fucking me in a storage room, kissing my neck when I should have been working. There was no recovering from this, and Tristan pulled back off me, walked around the shelving, and tugged his shorts up.

"James, wait. Please, please don't tell anybody," Tristan pleaded. James looked back and forth between us, flicking the light in the room on so he could see us better. The bulb sputtered to life, flickering and dim from lack of use. Hardly anybody bothered to turn on the light in there.

"You fucking lied, Connor," he said. Anger cut through his tone, and he took a step closer to me. "I can't believe I ever believed you when you said you hated him. You told me you didn't see how anybody could think he was hot, you told me you hated his guts, you told me he was a fucking idiot, and every bit of that was a lie?" He glared at me again, a look like he was trying to set me on fire.

Tristan eyed me; one eyebrow raised. With James's back to him, he couldn't see the shit-eating smirk on Tristan's face, the gotcha moment reading there as he found out just what I'd been saying behind his back. He wasn't angry. In fact, he seemed to be having trouble stifling a giggle over the contrast between what I'd said to others and things I'd told him, the way I'd tried so hard to hide what I felt from anyone who might put our...not-relationship...at risk. The things I said directly to him in bed, in the car, anytime we were together otherwise more than made up for my more public lies. And besides, it wasn't as if Tristan didn't know I hadn't always liked him.

"I'm sorry. I'm so sorry." I didn't even try to pretend I hadn't lied. At that point, why even try to tell him this wasn't anything, that it wasn't significant or important? What we had *was* a big deal and I was sick of denying that to everyone. Hell, I was sick of denying it to myself. Why try to hide the fact I thought Tristan was one of the sexiest humans I'd ever laid eyes on, once I got over how he could be such a dumbass sometimes? It was like he was cut from divine cloth, a gift from the gods with how good he looked. I couldn't pretend it wasn't true anymore. And I couldn't lie anymore and say I hated Tristan when I so obviously didn't. I could have tried to pretend what we did in the storage closet was a hatefuck, and tell James as much, try to defend this as some weird kind of hate and revenge sex. I easily could have. If I tried that, I knew my true feelings would shine in my voice, my real thoughts giving me away if I did. All I could do was apologize. "I'm sorry," I said again, but James just put his hand up. He didn't want to hear it.

Chapter Nineteen

I wasn't sorry I'd done it at all. I wasn't sorry for what Tristan and I had or what I'd let happen between us. I was happy for the first time in maybe forever. All I was sorry for was getting caught in the act, letting myself slip into the idea of getting fucked at work, into leaning hard into my carnal desires. But I wasn't sorry for what we'd done overall, not even remotely. I liked Tristan, cared about him on a deep, intense level I couldn't explain, and I wasn't about to apologize for how I felt or what I did. If being with him cost me my job, I was okay with that. Tristan would have been worth it, and I would have figured it out.

Tristan wasn't about that idea though. He went into overdrive to make things right, stepping toward me protectively like he wanted to defend what I was doing, but taking a step back like he knew I could handle it. James continued talking. "You know when I tell Greg you two have been fucking, he's going to fire you." *When,* not if. I wasn't even remotely surprised he'd tell Greg. The thing is, getting caught up with a patron was bad enough. That never used to be an issue, lifeguards dating people who came to the pool, but after two massive scandals with previous management, Greg swooped in and erred on the side of caution. The day he became manager, he banned any relationships with pool patrons altogether, for *all* employees. But Greg probably would have overlooked it, you know? If he'd found out that Tristan and I were having sex, that we were hooking up after work. We were both old enough, consenting, and Greg could only have so many rules against connections like this.

But the problem wasn't about that. It was so much worse. We had sex on pool property, during a time when I was supposed to be working. It was during my shift. I guess if we'd been smart enough to wait until my break, to take things to the car, maybe it would have been easier to defend myself against James. But we hadn't. I was supposed to be cleaning and instead I was getting myself impaled by a pool guest. It looked really bad because it *was* really bad.

"James, I'm seriously begging you, please. Don't tell him." Tristan was set on that, on saving my job for whatever reason. He looked at me almost apologetically and then turned back to James. "It was my fault. If you promise you'll keep quiet about it, I'll...I'll do anything you want." He looked at his feet, and I felt sick. James could ask for anything? It would be so easy for him to ask for me to quit, or for Tristan to leave the pool for good. I hated the thought of both of those things.

"Anything?" James took a step forward, looking at me out of the corner of his eye. "You'd really do anything to keep me from telling Greg you two are hooking up during Connor's shift?" He took another step closer to Tristan in a way that felt almost like a predator going after prey. He was the smallest of the three of us, but in that moment, he was powerful. His anger made him seem downright dangerous, and the way he kept moving toward Tristan was chilling and intense. I felt uneasy and sick to my stomach.

"Seriously, anything. Please don't tell him," Tristan agreed, and I could tell he was nervous when he said those words. I wondered if he would have taken back what he said if he knew what James was going to ask for, or if he'd have figured out a different agreement. James took a hard look at me and then turned back to Tristan again. And then, he kissed Tristan. He backed him against the wall, forcing his tongue into his mouth, and he grabbed his dick hard. Tristan didn't kiss back, but he did walk backward, letting James guide him so he wouldn't fall. Watching James do that hurt, and I wanted to step forward and kill him on the spot, but I was frozen in place.

"Fuck me like you fucked him," James said, making sure I heard exactly what he'd asked for. "You like that, Connor? Knowing your little boyfriend said he'd do anything, and now he has to fuck me?" Tristan didn't say anything.

"James, you don't want—" I started.

"Connor, get the fuck out of here and go clean the bathrooms," he said, impatient. "Unless you want to know how much better he'd be if he was with me. In that case, stay and watch how hot it is having him fuck me. I bet my hole is way tighter than yours could ever be. It's no secret you're a lying slut." He spat the words at me, and I looked at Tristan, trying to decipher the look he was giving me. I didn't know if it would be better to drop it now, to tell James to stop and to walk out of the door, tell Greg everything I'd done, or if I should do what James had asked.

"Hey, it's okay. Go," Tristan said. "It's okay, Connor. Trust me." I had no choice but to take his word for it, so I did what I had to. I picked up my bucket and I walked out of the storage room, leaving Tristan in there with James to pay for what I'd done, to sacrifice for the things we'd done together. I hated myself for the position I put him in because I couldn't just drop it.

All of this could have been different if I'd encouraged James more when it came to chasing Tristan, or if I'd somehow kept myself from hooking up with Tris in the first place. The situation could have been different if we'd avoided doing any of this at work too. And it could have been different if I'd been honest to begin with, I think, if I'd been up front about my interest in Tristan instead of lying through my teeth. Instead, I'd made my choices, and I'd thrown him to the wolves while I scrubbed a toilet and tried hard not to cry.

Chapter Twenty

I knew I needed to ask Tristan if he was okay after everything had happened. I knew I did, but when I was back on the stand, he was halfway across the pool. He wasn't looking over at me, and I didn't want to look too closely at him in case James caught me staring. I didn't see James, either, but that wasn't unexpected. We had started our day on opposite ends of the pool, and rotations had kept us apart aside from our ill-fated meeting in the storage room.

For a long while, it almost felt like Tristan was avoiding me, and the longer it went on that day, with me moving sections on my shift and Tristan moving to whichever section put the most distance between us, the more obvious it seemed. My paranoia kicked into overdrive. What if he'd liked what he did with James? What if he liked it better than the things we'd been doing all summer? What if his avoidance was an indicator of interest, that he'd moved on from me and into James?

I felt like an idiot for letting things happen how they had, ridiculous for ever letting me have feelings for him. I wasn't sure how much I believed in love, but in some way, I was falling for him, and I kicked myself for that. Everything would have been easier if I'd kept hating him like I did in the beginning, if I'd reminded myself daily of how stupid he'd been. In that moment, my self-loathing was strongest. All of this, every single part, was my fault, a downhill spiral as the result of my own stupid mistakes. My mind went to the worst places and considered the worst possibilities as I pictured them doing the things we did, as I considered Tristan and James making out in front of the gas station or getting burritos together or whatever else they could do. I tried not to think about them fucking.

At the end of the day, I almost considered walking off without even thinking about getting my stuff from my work locker. Even though he'd obviously gotten what he wanted, a part of me wondered if maybe James had told Greg after all. The last thing I really wanted was to be ambushed with a firing at the end of the day when I was barely holding it together in the first place. I mean, sure, if I was getting fired, I'd still get a phone call telling me not to come in, or be hit with the news in the morning, but that felt better than taking it right then. But my car keys were in my locker, and I didn't have a choice but to go there first. As I opened it, I could feel eyes on me. James was practically boring through me with his glare, so I turned and stared him down with more confidence than I thought I could have in me. Or, faked confidence, at least. "Yes?" I asked him. Part of me hadn't wanted to engage in any kind of conversation, but it was obvious he wasn't planning to stop his stare down until I did.

"You can keep your job," he said, slamming his locker door and shoving past me, his shoulder hitting mine as he did. I muttered a "thanks," but he was already out of earshot. When I got to my car, I was ready for the day to be over. I wanted to go home, curl up in bed, and bury my head in my pillow. All the stress felt like too much, and my fears that Tristan had fucked him and enjoyed it were far too present.

"You always leave your car unlocked?" Tristan's voice made me jump out of my skin. I was so focused on my thoughts and the frustrated sort of way I felt, I wasn't thinking about checking my car or anything. I was lucky it was Tristan in the passenger seat and not James, who was mad at me for whatever reason instead of being thankful for the chance my fuck-up had given him. Before having that leverage, he didn't have a shot in hell, and as far as I knew, he'd gotten everything he wanted.

"I thought I locked it," I said. I didn't want to look at him, like the way he'd been dodging me all day and how he wanted to talk as soon as work was over didn't bode well for what we had going. It was easy to assume this was the end of the line for our little hookup, and for whatever reason, I was incredibly sad over that. He rested his hand on my arm and I resisted the urge to pull away from his touch. I was sure this was his way of letting me down easy and I felt so small.

"What's wrong?" he asked me, letting his fingers rub where his hand had been resting moments before.

"Nothing. Thanks for saving my job." I was afraid if I said anything more, it would be apparent I was upset, more upset than I should have been for what the thing we had together was supposed to be, and if anything I should have been thankful and not upset anyway. He'd done me a favor.

"You're not happy," he said. It was a statement and not a question, so I knew he knew I was upset, but I looked away from him, afraid to confirm it. "Oh my God, Connor, are you jealous?" He sounded genuinely surprised by his discovery, like he didn't think I could be jealous knowing he fucked someone else. Not that I had any right to be—hell, I'd fucked someone else, and this wasn't even a thing—but that didn't mean I could control how I felt. I couldn't switch off the feelings I had for Tristan.

"I'm not," I insisted. I still couldn't look at him.

"Holy crap, you're actually jealous of James? Babe!" The term of endearment felt like a little much. We didn't use them too often with each other, and it startled me, in the kind of way that made me wish it weren't out of place at all.

"Whatever, it's...it's not a big deal. I mean, you're allowed to fuck anyone you want, and...and you saved my job anyway, so just forget it." I was annoyed with myself for sounding so obvious and for letting my voice crack as I choked back tears.

"Mmm, okay, Mister Jealousy. You really want to tell me you didn't fuck anyone else this summer?" He dipped his head low to catch my eyes, and I looked out of the corner of them at him, seeing his smirk like he'd caught my hand in the cookie jar.

"Fine, okay. I hooked up with somebody a couple of times when you weren't like...when you weren't around. Is that what you want to hear? That we're somehow equal now?" I didn't know why I was so defensive about it, or why I was so mad. The two weren't even situations that could be equated at all. I fucked Alex because I wanted to, because I needed someone to fuck, and he was there. He fucked James to keep my job for me. But for some reason, I felt the sting of jealousy all the same.

"I knew it," he said. He winked and put a hand on my face, trying to turn my head to look at him. "See? It's okay. I'm only a little jealous." His hand didn't leave my face, so I turned to look at him more like he wanted.

"I haven't fucked anybody else lately," I promised. I didn't know why I was promising that. It sounded a little ridiculous, a little too revealing, and I second-guessed it as soon as the words left my mouth. He didn't need to know I was only after him. I didn't want to show all my cards that easily.

"Oh, I know," he told me. "I mean, you're insatiable, but I'm pretty sure you don't need that much extra given how much we've been, you know..." He poked his forefinger through a circle made with his other hand. He was right. We made a lot of time for each other after work, in the morning, whenever we could. "Anyway, I didn't fuck him."

"What?" Given the fact James said I still had my job, that was impossible for me to believe. Not that I didn't trust him, but...*what?* My brain couldn't seem to make sense of how he'd managed to help me without helping James out.

"Seriously. Oh gosh, babe, did you actually think I was going to?" He watched my face go through a range of emotions, and suddenly he got dead serious. "Oh gosh, I'm...I'm so sorry. You...God, Connor, you didn't know I wasn't ever going to?" It was only just dawning on him then that I hadn't realized his intentions at all, that I assumed when he asked me to leave, he wanted me to give them the time and space to do what James so desperately wanted them to do.

"You avoided me all day. I assumed..." I started to explain.

"I stayed out of your section because I didn't really want to add insult to injury with James. It probably wouldn't have helped the job situation for me to tell him I wouldn't fuck him, and then come over to your section and flirt all day right in front of him. That would have been really shitty. And I would've left, but I wanted to talk to you after work."

"I...I really thought you...I don't know, just forget it,"
I said. But then my curiosity got the best of me and I
couldn't let it die. "Seriously, though, what do you mean
you didn't fuck him?" I wondered if maybe he'd given in
partially, let James have an inch in hopes he wouldn't take
a mile, if he'd found middle ground, maybe sucked his
dick like he had mine to make me less angry at him. I don't
know why I needed or wanted to know, but I did. Maybe I
just liked torturing myself.

"I mean we didn't do anything, Connor. He was
obviously going to crumble at the slightest pushback once
I got him alone." He saw things in James I didn't see. To
me, James was dead set on them hooking up, and I don't
know what he was able to pinpoint that said otherwise.

"What do you mean?" I repeated myself. I needed to
know.

"I mean he's a virgin, Connor. I wasn't going to take
that from him in a half-assed attempt to get laid, not like
that. The whole immaturity angle was written all over
him, that manipulative little 'if I don't make someone fuck
me, I'll never get laid' insecurity sort of thing." He read
James so much differently than I had. In the way I saw
him as strong and forceful, a terrifying predator, he saw
him as vulnerable and weak, easily squashed like a bug.

"So, what happened, then?" I asked. I didn't know for
sure that I wanted to pull the information from him.
Maybe not knowing was better. But I couldn't wrap my
brain around how Tristan had saved my job without
hooking up with James. I couldn't understand.

"As soon as I saw his angle, I had you leave. And then
I let him get close to me. We did kiss, that happened. He
was starting to get flustered from it. I don't think he's ever
been that close before, really, to getting laid or whatever.

I asked him why he wanted it so badly, and he got really defensive, asking why I'd fuck you when you hate me and not fuck him when he loves me, and that made it a whole hell of a lot clearer to me."

"Loves you? Have you two even exchanged more than like, five words?"

"Not really. He's young and confused, babe," Tristan said. Part of me wanted him to stop calling me that because the pet name affected me way more than it should have. The other part of me wanted him to say it again and again forever. "He's mixing up love and lust and all that other shit, basically. It happens. Anyway, I asked if this was really how he wanted this to happen—if he actually wanted to do this in a smelly supply closet. And then I called him out on his virgin nature and said this wasn't how he wanted to lose it; with someone he didn't know in a place like this. I went for the emotional angle, and I told him he deserved better than that." He smiled sadly, like he felt bad for crushing James's heart, even if it was necessary.

"And it worked?" I asked. I mean, obviously it had worked, but it seemed surprising to me that James would back down so quickly.

"He's a scared kid, Connor. He's what, eighteen? I've been there. I've tried manipulating and bribery to get laid the first time."

Manipulation? I furrowed my brow. "Oh my God, did I...?" I felt horrified at the prospect that I might have been his first without realizing it.

Instead, Tristan busted out laughing. "Are you kidding? No, not you. Did I seem that inexperienced to you? Jesus. I was a tutor. And by that, I mean I wrote half of the football team's English papers while getting really up close and personal with them as payment," he told me. I shouldn't have been surprised he was running that sort of racket in school, some kind of head-for-brains exchange that apparently worked well for him. "Anyway, it's not that, uh, fulfilling for someone to fuck you because they have to. I think he'll figure that out eventually. Hopefully not before he finds out the hard way." He clearly spoke from experience.

"Yeah, I mean...yeah..." I didn't want to let on how relieved I was. That seemed so childish, to be so over-the-top excited about the fact they didn't bang. I was frustrated. I wondered which part mattered more to me: that Tristan didn't pay for my choices, or that Tristan wasn't with anyone else when I cared for him so strongly. Either one was a problem.

"You're still not happy," Tristan said, reaching over to play with the hair on the nape of my neck. I resisted the urge to shudder. He knew all too well how that spot affected me, and we weren't done talking about this.

"I'm fine. I just don't get what made him drop it so easily, is all." That wasn't entirely true. The underlying fear was still there. If I got fired, whatever, I got fired. I'd figure something else out. But I still worried James would be pissed, that he'd somehow retaliate, and more than that, I worried Tristan was making some kind of massive mistake, mostly for getting mixed up with me to begin with. I didn't like the thought of him getting hurt because I was a fuck-up. That should have been my biggest clue that I was in way too deep.

"Connor, he thought he was going to be able to bully someone into having sex with him. He probably thought you and I were just some quick hookup and it was something he could get in on. The second he realized that

I actually care about you, he backed off. He's not going to fuck with your job. Trust me." He was so sure James was done, and I wasn't, but I was still hung up on the part where Tristan said he cared about me. "Come on, let's go get Slurpees and get that pretty little head of yours back where it belongs," Tristan said, leaning over and kissing my jaw. He didn't give me any opportunity to ask him to elaborate on the part where he said he cared about me. In hindsight, I'm pretty sure the subject change was on purpose, but he said we should go get Slurpees, so we did.

The next time we kissed, his tongue was purple and mine was green. It was slow and lazy, like we had all the time in the world, and for at least a few moments, we did. "You're still in your head, pretty boy," he said. I wondered how he knew by a kiss alone. That was the problem. Tristan knew me too well.

"Fuck you," I said quietly, not like I was upset, but like I was annoyed he'd caught me.

He just smirked. "You'd really like that, wouldn't you?" he asked me. Then he placed his hand on top of mine on the gearshift. "Go on, then. Drive. Let's go see if this Slurpee tongue gives you a purple dick."

Chapter Twenty-One

The next time Tristan drew a portrait of me, I didn't know he was drawing me. I was at work, standing there, whistle resting on my lower lip, held there just barely by my curled top one. Those were the details he captured of me, the focused look in my eyes and the hand resting on my hip. He caught the way my swim trunks wrinkled, probably from being tossed on my floor unceremoniously the day before when we'd hooked up. And he caught the shaggy way my hair fell and how my sunglasses held it in place. He noticed the way my guard tube's strap left a red mark on my back if it was in the same place for too long. I had no idea he was drawing me. I knew he was sitting out of the water that afternoon, sketching, but I didn't know the way he was focused on me, paying attention to every last detail, capturing it on the page in front of him. He saw things in me I didn't. He saw things in everyone I didn't, just like he'd seen the insecurity in James, but in me, he saw a strength I didn't think I had, an authority I wasn't sure I was in full command of, and it left me in awe. When he showed me the portrait later, I was speechless.

"Why do you draw me?" I asked him. "You're so talented, and you...you spent that time focused on me." There were so many better things he could draw, so many better people to look at. I didn't understand why me, why my face and body and features.

"I like what you look like. And I like getting that on a page so I can remember it later. I don't want to forget this." That part hit me like a knife, and I wanted to cry. I didn't want to forget it, either, but I didn't have the talent to get it down in a drawing, to keep what we had safe on paper forever. I didn't have a way of preserving what we had like he did, but I had the same desperate need to do that.

That day, I offered him the other half of my hot dog. I had to get back on the stand, and he hadn't eaten. But Tristan's situation was worse for him than he was letting on. That was the thing about Tristan. What bothered me most about him was how he was twice as self-assured as me. Nothing fazed him. Just as he'd met his dad kicking him out with a shrug and a small laugh, he'd met my concern about him spending the night in the park like it was nothing. It was the day after I'd given him half of my hot dog, and he'd texted me asking if I wanted to meet him at the park. I had an unexpected day off, since Greg had somehow accidentally scheduled two too many guards. The bench at the park wasn't comfortable enough for us to sit and eat ice cream without my butt going numb. There was no way it was comfortable enough for him to sleep on. "Seriously," I pleaded. "Come over tonight. Alex can't get mad if it's been a while and if it's just for the night. We can pretend like you came over to watch a movie and we fell asleep."

"You're too loud when you get fucked for that to be a compelling argument, pretty boy," he said. He'd taken to calling me that again, the name that had gotten under my skin at the beginning of summer now sending shivers down my spine in a good way. "Better off telling him I came over and we fell asleep after and forgot."

"I don't care what we tell him. I just don't want you to sleep on a park bench tonight," I said. The worry was apparent in my voice. "Isn't there something we can do about it? Will your dad let you come back?"

"I'm not asking him. He'll call when he's ready," he told me.

"He needs help, Tris," I told him. Letting him do this on a cycle wasn't helping anyone, particularly not Tristan, who had college to get through and everything else. If I weren't locked into my lease, I'd have convinced him to find a place we could rent together. Not even in a "let's move in together" kind of way, even if that wasn't a terrible idea, but in a "you can't sleep on park benches every night" kind of way. But I was locked in, and what I needed was for his dad to get help so he could go home.

"Some people don't want to be helped," he told me. "Some people want to be left to wallow in it." His voice said a lot. It wasn't like he was unwilling to help his dad, not the way I'd thought. The tone was a tired one, one that had tried a lot and likely failed. My heart ached for him but talking about it now wasn't doing anyone any good.

"Okay," I said. I didn't know where else to take the conversation from there. The dark stain on our talks seemed to mark them, to make it harder to move past them and talk about something lighter, for me at least.

For Tristan, yet again, it didn't faze him. "Hey, I've got a way to cheer you up. You promised me a certain excuse for me to stay over, and your ass isn't going to fill itself," he said, watching as I stood up and tossed the last few bites of my ice cream cone in the nearby trash can. As I turned back to him, he took a step closer. He tangled his fingers in my hair with one hand and grabbed my ass with the other before giving it a small slap. "Let's get you home." Now that James knew, it didn't matter as much to me for us to be as quiet about things. Besides, we were halfway across town from the pool as it was. Greg wasn't going to catch us there.

The third time Tristan drew me, it wasn't a drawing of all of me. It was just of my cock. Mostly, it was a drawing of Tristan. When we'd gotten to my room, we found ourselves in the same position we'd been in at the park, this time with me against the door. His hand was on my ass and the other was pulling my hair, and he tilted my head back to get his mouth on my collarbones. That day, he wasn't shy about leaving marks. I didn't care—I'd wear a swim shirt the next day if I had to. The moment was worth it, the hickeys and love bites dotting my neck and upper chest. "Fuck me," I said, my need evident in the way I pressed against his thigh, hard and pleading.

"I will, pretty boy. Give me some time." He liked to take his time, to give me a whole heck of a lot more than I needed to get going. I don't know why he took it so slowly so much of the time, but I wasn't complaining about it. He walked me back to the bed, pushed me back onto the sheets, and dipped his head so he could kiss me. "I have an idea."

Tristan's idea, or him saying he had one, should have scared me. I mean, he could be unpredictable, and his big ideas had taken us to some pretty rough places—him faking a drowning, us fucking at work. But for some crazy fucking reason, I trusted him. If he would have told me, "Listen, Connor, the only way I'll fuck you is if you go get your dick pierced," I would have.

"What's your idea?" I asked him, breath heavy from how he was laying on me, kissing my jaw.

"Let me draw you?" he asked me.

"Now?" In the middle of foreplay seemed like the worst time, or maybe it was the best time, a certain mood or spirit he wanted to capture, and I needed to know what he wanted, why he wanted it. My answer didn't mean no, and it didn't mean wait. I just wanted to know what was in his head.

"You say that like you don't think you can stay hard long enough," he told me. He kissed his way down my body, slid my shorts down, kissed the top of my thigh. "Come on, I want to try this."

"Can't you take a reference photo and fuck me, then draw me?" I asked him, groaning. He was going to make me wait forever, I was sure.

"It'll be better this way. Trust me, the light is perfect right now. Jesus, Connor, you're a work of art, I swear to God." He slid off me, grabbed his sketchpad and some pencils out of his bag, and then climbed back onto the bed. "I really want to draw your cock," he insisted, smile curling on his lips.

"Just my cock?" I asked. Usually it felt like Tristan was about the full picture, about the whole body, the whole scene, and today, he seemed set on focusing, details, one little part of me.

"Trust me. I think you'll like this one." He propped himself up so he could stroke my dick and get me really hard. I was aching. And then he held me there, sketching, placing his lips on the side of my cock and then letting go to draw for a moment, before coming back to it, same position, his mouth on me, his hands on me. It was the weirdest form of edging, the strangest thing he could do to get me all worked up and turned on and confused as hell. I wanted to come. My balls throbbed and ached for me to get off already. But I was interested in what he was doing, and he made it clear looking was off-limits. "I'll show you after," he promised me, nudging my hands and face away from trying to see. "Hold still."

I did what he said. I'd have done anything he said. And it only took him about half an hour to get what he was getting, the base drawing he was going for. When he set his sketchpad down, I asked if he was done, and the smirk he had told me no, no he wasn't. He kissed my stomach and looked up at me.

"Done enough that I think I can really, really make sure you know how much I appreciate you letting me do that," he told me. His tongue lapped at the hollow places between my hip bones and lower abs, the areas that were lean and exposed, and I moaned, rolling my hips up more to meet his tongue. "You're such a good model for me, babe. You're so fucking good for me."

"I need you," I told him, not responding to his praise because I still didn't know how to react to it when it seemed so unwarranted and undeserved. He smiled at me, teased me with his hands as he made his way up my body to kiss me.

"Take me anyway you want me, Connor. I'm all yours. Tell me how you want it." His earnest tone sent chills through me. I had literal goose bumps from it. I pulled him close and kissed him. I didn't know what I wanted. I wanted everything. I wanted to freeze time just like this. I wanted more. I wanted him in me.

"Can we start just like this?" I asked, holding him close to me and hooking a leg around his waist. "I want to see you."

We'd done this a whole hell of a lot of ways, and it was all him holding me, him on me, him covering me every way he could. But I wanted him to face me, for our bodies to be wholly together and aligned and intense. He was perfect, and I needed to feel that. "I love that idea," he half-breathed on my lips. "I've been waiting for you to ask."

It never occurred to me that he was waiting for me to ask for anything. After all, he'd always taken charge in things. But then I realized once again, my perception wasn't necessarily the reality there, that perhaps he'd taken the lead solely because I'd failed to. It was as if he filled those spaces in me, not just physically but emotionally, guiding me because I was too afraid to guide him. There were things we hadn't done because I hadn't thought to ask, hadn't told him how much I wanted to have him just like this, his chest on mine, his body against and in and on and around me. I wanted to feel him and see him and *know* him in ways that might not have even been possible.

When he entered me, my leg was on his shoulder, but he moved it. I may have asked him to take me like that, but he directed my movements with soft touches and gentle kisses.

"You're so good, Connor, so beautiful..." he'd mutter between thrusts, and I'd whimper and tell him how amazing he felt in me. His teeth tugged at my lower lip as he pushed into me, again, again, *again*. Each thrust reverberated in me, amplified by the way he looked at me, the way he talked to me, the way his hands held me, wrapped around me, grasping my shoulders to pull me down onto his cock every time he thrust up into me.

"I'm so close," he told me. "I can't...I have to come, baby..." he said, almost as if he was frustrated by his own need for release, and then I could feel him, could feel the way he tensed and the way his chest rattled with his grunts and it was everything I wanted. That was enough for me, heaven captured in a moment. As soon as he came, his hands were on me, stroking me as he pushed into me a few more times. I could tell by the way he shook that he was tense, overwhelmed, a little overstimulated by everything. My own orgasm followed right after, not taking long at all, not with the way he was encouraging me, not with the way he felt and the way his body moved and how he looked at me. He fed me my own come with his fingers, swiping it off my stomach and his chest before running those fingers on my lips, and I tasted it. When he kissed me, I was sure he did, too, certain he tasted the impact of what he'd done to me and how amazing it felt.

"Connor, you're a work of art," he told me again. It was the second time he'd told me that. Then he settled beside me and picked up his sketchpad. I was still naked and exposed, even with him half-draping the sheets on us, if only for warmth now that our bodies weren't on each other. I leaned my head on his shoulder then, watched as his drawing came to life with details he hadn't added on the first sweep.

It was what could be best described as a self-portrait. Sure, it was my dick in the drawing, but it was his face, his lips, his collarbones in frame. He drew the ripples of my shorts bunched by his chest, shadowed the curves of his bones and muscles deep and dark to match his tan. His lips were kissable, plush and soft on the page, just like in real life, and I felt a deep ache to interrupt him, to kiss those same lips. Thankfully, he let me, turning to kiss me any time I asked and then returning to what he was doing.

"You should go to an art school," I told him. "You're really good at that."

"Can you imagine? Me at an art school? Getting my own studio display night and hanging your cock on the wall? Connor, you'd be famous, you'd be actual art," he said, chuckling, nosing at my hair and kissing the top of my head. "It's a nice dream."

"You could make it real," I told him. I didn't get why he'd settle, why he'd go somewhere that had nothing emphasizing the arts, engineering, anything he wanted to do at all. He could do amazing things, and he was making a choice not to, deciding he didn't want to go for a dad who didn't want him at all.

"Connor, none of that's real. I mean, it's not something I can just *do*. It isn't that easy." To me, it seemed exactly that easy. I'd left home in search of my dream, gone states away for a better nursing school than the one in my own state. What he wanted—*really* wanted—could have been real, and he could have done it. My heart broke for the lack of confidence he had in his future, and, for a moment, I wondered if that was how he felt anytime he complimented me.

"I don't want to see you settle," I told him.

"You know if I stay, we could..." He paused for a moment, penciling in the shine on a drop of precome. "Never mind," he finished with.

Neither of us wanted to say it, to put words to what this was, what our connection could be if he stayed in town. If we defined it, there was no going back. I mean, if we said the words, there was a chance we'd have to eventually un-say them. That was the scary part I didn't want to consider. It wasn't that un-saying them was a bad thing at all. Instead, we both seemed to feel that if we did this, if we spoke words to what we had, there was a chance we would break everything. Whatever we had, there was some sort of fragility in it, like we were stealing time to make this happen. So even if he stayed, saying what this was if it could be anything was too much.

Sometimes I wonder if my driving factor to tell him he should go to another school was about him, and my desire for him to have the best, or if it was selfish, if it was about me being scared of what we might have if he was right there. What we were was only supposed to be a summer fling, or really, it was never supposed to be anything at all and then it *was* a summer fling. That afternoon was the first time I'd stopped to consider the idea that because it had gone from nothing to a summer fling, maybe it could go from being a summer fling to something more. I kicked myself for letting my mind go there.

His sketch was beautiful. Not because he'd done an amazing job of drawing my dick, but because it captured the very essence of what we had together. His eyes sparkled, and I'm not sure how he'd made them do that considering he only had charcoal pencils to work with, but they did. And he did. He shone on the page as much as he did in person, such a vibrant, radiant being. I told him as much, and he tore the art out of his sketchbook. "Keep it," he said. "I don't want you to forget this either." I could feel the lump in my throat.

Round two was faster, more frenzied, less careful and reverent. Round two had us tangled, had sheets wrapped between and around and on us. Round two took only minutes, hands and mouths and bodies moving, not so much desperate to come as wanting to connect all over again. There wasn't a drawing to slow us down this time. The moment held us; us and the little time we had left. We could have had eternity and in that second, it wouldn't have felt like enough, and we hurried as a result.

That night, sex-spent and comfortable, I fell asleep in his arms, the drawing he'd made me on my dresser held down by the edge of the lamp, fluttering a little bit every time the fan oscillated from the foot of the bed to the head of it. Being with him felt safe. I'd never slept more soundly than I did that night as he held me closely.

Chapter Twenty-Two

I slept through my class. It was a mistake, but thankfully I hadn't missed a single day so far that summer, so there was no real emergency. I could always text someone for notes or whatever. The darkness of the morning was to blame for me oversleeping, I think, the way the storm clouds had rolled in overnight and poured, trailing streaks of water down my windows and a darkness in the clouds that felt like early morning, not like time to be awake at all. The rain puddled near my car outside. I could see it from the window, the nasty weather, the lightning streaks, and once I realized I wasn't making it to class on time, Tristan had me convinced to stay in bed just like we'd been doing. My phone buzzed with a text from Greg saying the pool was closing for the day. The storms were too heavy to open, and even if they cleared, there was no guarantee that guards could get there without warning later. My day was free. I could lock myself in my room with Tristan on top of me. Spending the day like that was all I wanted.

Sex sustained us through early afternoon, and anytime we took breaks, we laid in bed and talked. He rubbed my back and played with my hair, and I kissed his chest and stomach and laid across his body, picking at stray threads on my sheets. That day was the best one of my summer to that point. We didn't leave the bed until our stomachs growled and protested, begging for food. Burgers seemed like a good way to remedy that need.

We'd agreed on just one night, if nothing else but for Alex's sake, to get around him being upset about Tristan overstaying his welcome again. But one more night didn't seem like too much to ask as I fed Tristan a French fry, dipped in my favorite mayo-ketchup combo. He'd been grossed out until he tasted my concoction and then he was sold, licking the excess off my fingers in ways that made me want to climb in his lap in the middle of a burger place. "Stay over again," I pleaded. I wasn't asking, though. I was begging, near-insisting on it.

"Alex will be mad," he said.

"I don't care. Please?" I asked him. I needed another night. I was desperate.

"Okay. I need to go check on my dad though. I haven't heard from him in a few days. And I need some clean clothes," he told me. It was a change from the previous day, when I'd asked him to call and he'd said no. This time, he seemed worried.

"You think he'll let you in?" I asked. I didn't really know how the dynamic worked when Tristan was kicked out; if it was okay for him to dip back in for clothes and stuff whenever.

"I don't know. I guess if he doesn't, I'll run to the store and pick up some tank tops or whatever, but I'm gonna try. He's usually at least texted by now." There was something sad in Tristan's voice, in the way his face fell talking about it. I worried I'd struck a nerve by asking, but if he needed to go, it made sense that he should.

"You want me to drive? I can stay in the car if you need," I offered. "I mean, obviously if you want me to take you. I don't have to. Or I could drop you off. Or—" I was rambling. I didn't know how to make him look less sad and I hated that. I just wanted to help, and I didn't know how. I felt useless.

"I'd love a ride, Connor. Thanks. Gimme another one of those fries?" he asked, nodding toward my basket, and I picked one up, dipped it again, and lifted it to his lips. I'd feed him fries forever if it meant his mind wasn't on things that hurt him. I'd buy a million more baskets of them; I'd do whatever it took. He only deserved good things. Realizing that had taken me far too long, and I'd spend the rest of summer trying to prove to him that I knew it now, to apologize for it taking me so long to sort it out to begin with.

On the drive over, he was quiet. The skies were still gray, still threatening to spill over with more rain, and I wondered if we'd end up having another day off work the next day. If we did, I was skipping class again, spending the day the same way as this one. I wanted to soak up all the time I possibly could with him. I didn't want to waste that time in class if I didn't have to.

He held my hand, rubbing it with his thumb. "You can come in with me if you want. He'll probably just yell at me, let me get my stuff, and go."

"Do you want me to go in? I can," I asked. I wasn't sure if he said it because he thought I'd hate waiting in the car, or if he said I could come in because he genuinely wanted me with him, so I played it safe. I'd do anything he wanted.

"I want you with me," he said.

"I'm there, then. I'll be there," I told him, patting his hand and rubbing the back of his neck to reassure him. I had his back; I had his everything he needed me to have then.

Five minutes.

Tristan knocked for five minutes with no response. He rang the doorbell again and again...nothing.

"I don't get why he isn't answering," he said. "His car is in the driveway. I don't get it." I could see the frustration, the fear, the panic on his face. I wanted to shake him, to kiss him, to tell him it would be okay, but fuck, I didn't know for sure that it would, honestly. How did I know his dad didn't know he was there and was ignoring him intentionally? I didn't know how to reassure him when I couldn't be positive what was happening or why his dad wouldn't answer the door. I didn't know. I was angry. Not at Tristan but at a father who would be so uncaring as to not open the door for his son, even if Tristan wasn't his. He'd raised him, and in my mind, he should have been there for him.

"Maybe he's sleeping or something. He might not be able to hear you." I was trying to be reassuring, trying not to let my anger seep through. "Or maybe he went for a walk." I didn't want to say what seemed obvious to me: maybe he was too drunk to move.

"Maybe," he said. I could tell he didn't believe my words, that the thoughts I was having were on his mind too. He fished a key from his pocket. If he'd had a key all along, I wondered why we had been standing outside for five minutes trying to get his dad's attention. "I didn't want to use this," he said. "I thought he'd let me in." I nodded. He started to put the key in the slot, but then knocked again, harder and louder, pounding at the door until heavy drops of rain fell from the sky. It was the feeling of the water on his skin that led him to turn the key in the lock and push his way in. He gripped my hand as he put the key back into his pocket. "Come on."

I followed. The house was dim, and the wallpaper peeled. A light in the living room was switched on, I thought. I could see the glow from the mud room we started in, and as Tristan led me through the kitchen, past the table with a plate still sitting there, past the refrigerator humming, we didn't hear a sound. "Dad?" he called. "I'm just grabbing some clothes, and then I'll leave, promise." No answer. "Dad?" Those were the last seconds of normalcy, the last moment before things shattered.

It was broken glass, I think, that Tristan saw first. Or maybe that's what I saw first. I'm not sure. It was at the ground at his dad's feet, the liquid long evaporated. I couldn't tell you how many days he'd been there: if it had been one or four or seven. Tristan hadn't been there in well over a week, and his absence wasn't by his own choosing. I don't know if it was better or worse that he hadn't been there, if it would have been better for him to wake up to it the next morning, or if it was better for him to come home to see, to know what had happened wasn't his fault. And it wasn't Tristan's fault. It was his dad's own doing. He poured himself a drink. He sat down. He died. Tristan couldn't have stopped that, couldn't have done anything to change it. I know that. I'm not sure in that moment Tristan knew that.

Things were kind of a blur. I still can't remember them clearly, thinking back on it. I remember there was a brick frame near the fireplace, a raised area one could sit on to be close to the flames. The fireplace was unlit of course, in the dead of summer, but the brick still made a perfect seat. Tristan sat down and curled up in a ball there, drawing his knees to his chest.

"What do I even do?" he asked me. "I mean, am I supposed to call someone?"

"The police?" I asked. I didn't know.

"What do we tell them? That my dad's been dead for days? That's not really an emergency," he told me. He was right. Calling 9-1-1 about it didn't make sense. We weren't in any sort of emergency. What happened was done and it just...was. A fly landed on his dad's finger, giving more gravity to the fact that we were too late. I think it would have been too late regardless, but the presence of life on something so dead made it even clearer. The fly buzzed with movement, crawling up his hand.

"What about the non-emergency number?" That was always an option. He nodded, burying his face in his knees. He wasn't crying, didn't shake or sob or anything else. He just sat there. He stayed sitting there while I made the call, stayed where he was as the coroner stood over his dad's body. He'd answer questions, tell the truth—he wasn't there, hadn't been there, came back to get clothes and found him—and we waited. He signed papers. I sat with him, wrapped my arms around him. He still didn't cry. Not yet. Not right then. I don't know if he felt like he had to stay strong because I was there, or if he was trying to act mature in the face of this as people moved his dad, took him with them, or if he was in shock. I didn't know, but he sat there, and I held him, and he clung to my arm with one hand so hard it left marks of the imprints of his fingers that lasted for days. I didn't mind.

Everyone asked if he had plans, funeral arrangements, if his dad had done any end-of-life planning. He shook his head. "I don't even know what to do," he told me a little bit after things died down. I didn't really know what to do either. I'd never lost anyone close to me. I mean, this was new territory, the idea that now there were things to do. I had experience with death, and

I had experience with saving lives, to some degree or another, or at least had a little bit of medical training under my belt. Neither of those things applied here. I didn't know what to do with someone who was already dead. I couldn't bring him back for Tristan. I couldn't make it better. I felt helpless.

"Does he have an office? I can go look and see if he left behind any sort of instructions or plans or a will or something," I told him. Tristan wasn't in the state of mind to be doing that kind of thing. It wasn't fair to encourage him to go look and dig through his dad's belongings anyway. God knows what he'd find.

"It's up the hall." He nodded in the right direction. He barely let go of my arm, and I sat with him a few more minutes before trying to get free of his grasp to go look.

"I'll be right back," I promised, giving him a small kiss on the shoulder. Tristan hadn't directed me where to go specifically. "Up the hall" didn't give me much to go on when there were doorways on doorways, most closed. I started with the first one, peeking in and seeing a bathroom. I closed that one right away. The second room, though, obviously wasn't the office. I went in anyway.

I hadn't ever seen the room before, hadn't ever expected to, but I could have picked it out of a lineup, could have told anyone it was Tristan's room from a mile away. It screamed of his personality, his talent, and the things he was most interested in. While my childhood room held swimming trophies and whatever color my mom was most interested in at that moment, Tristan's room was clearly his own. It was mostly tidy, outside of a small heap of laundry in a corner, spilling out of the hamper next to it. The walls had a soft blue color to them, like muted skies on a day that wasn't quite rainy or sunny, but just *was*. But against the near wall, it was immediately obvious where he spent most of his time: at a desk smudged with charcoal and pastels and dotted with paint. Sketching clearly wasn't his only medium, but it was his preferred one, and that was apparent by the number of sketches taped to the wall above his desk. There were some paintings mixed in, but the sketches stood out strongest.

I thought I knew every drawing Tristan had done of me. I was wrong. There were more, some moments he'd captured when I hadn't realized it. There was one of me sleeping, and I wondered if one night when he'd stayed, he'd been sleepless and decided to sketch instead. I looked softer than I did in real life, more peaceful than I'd felt in years. That was probably his doing. In another, there were only hands, but given the theme of the rest of them, I could assume one of the hands was mine. They were interlocked, clearly done from memory because I'd never seen him draw our hands before, not like this. I looked at my own hands and then back at the picture, the sketch of hands clasped the same way we'd have them anytime he was in my car. There was another of our legs, tangled in sheets. I hadn't seen him draw this one, either, but it was clearly my legs with his. He'd captured the freckle on my ankle and the one on my big toe. The final one was different from the others, less guarded and soft. It was me, gripping the sheets, face twisted with what could only be described as beautiful, passionate agony. The point of view allowed me to see through his eyes for a moment, to see the lines and curves of my body the way he did, to see what he saw when he was making love to me. There was something too intense, too careful about the drawing to refer to it as one where he was fucking me. No, there was a longing behind it, feelings that meant something. Feelings I hadn't been ready to speak a name to, but couldn't deny, not when they were looking me in the face. He saw it, too, saw the things I couldn't tell him.

As I backed out of his room and quietly closed the door again to find the office, I realized two things: One, I was more thankful than I could express over how he'd taken time to capture what we had together. For me, this felt like memories I might forget, but for him, there were tangible reminders lining his walls. Even if he took them down, discarded them, did whatever with them after this summer, he found these moments worth preserving, worth putting on paper, and that tugged at me in a way I can't fully explain. Two, I could never, ever tell him I'd found the drawings or his room. In my mind, there was a reason he'd never shown me those things, never told me they existed, and telling him when he was already vulnerable and afraid seemed cruel. I decided to thank him silently and to pretend I'd never seen it at all. Anything more seemed like an invasion of sorts.

The office was a sharp contrast to the tidiness of his room. The trash bin was full to the point of overflowing, wadded paper on the floor around the desk. A few bills were stacked there, marked *overdue*. I felt compelled to look at the checkbook beside the bills, if only to see how much trouble Tristan might be in. Now with his father gone, the bills would likely be his responsibility to pay, and if the checkbook showed empty accounts, he'd be fucked. There was money, though, more than enough to cover the bills at least, if not much extra to help him by. The overdue bills weren't down to a lack of money, that was for sure. His dad simply hadn't paid them for whatever reason. I'm assuming the empty glass on the desk played a role in why he hadn't bothered. But financially, there was enough for now, which was what mattered.

The top desk drawer revealed a leather-bound notebook. I wanted to look in it, to see what it contained, but I was nervous. I didn't know Tristan's father, not even remotely, and to peek into his private thoughts seemed dangerous. But I wasn't sure Tristan was in the frame of mind to come back here himself, to sift through it, and I feared it might contain something that would only hurt him. If that was the case, I didn't want him to know the notebook existed, or at least, I didn't want him to know right now, not when he was so vulnerable, and his emotions were so raw. I opened it and flipped back to front in hopes of finding the last written page. Half of the notebook was blank.

Tristan,

I don't know why I keep writing these notes to you instead of telling you to your face. Truth be told, I'll probably toss this one in the fireplace when I'm done, just like I did with the others. But the truth is, you've been trying to help me for years and it's not getting anywhere, is it? Maybe some people can't be helped, buddy. That's not your fault. It's mine. We both know I haven't been the same since we lost her. You haven't, either, and that's okay. I'm still proud of you.

One of these days we'll figure it out, but don't worry. You're still my son.

Dad

Pages and pages were just like that, apologies, notes, stories about Tristan's mom. My heart ached for the fact that Tristan would never have all of them. After all, his dad had burned them, and it was only in his passing that this one hadn't gone into the fire too. But it held hope, too, the hope that Tristan wasn't as unloved as he might have felt when his dad kicked him out each time, and he needed to see what his dad truly felt. He needed to know his dad loved him more than he could actually tell him. As much as I disliked the man for how he'd made Tris feel, we were alike in that way...more feelings than we could fully express to him. I tucked the leather-bound volume under my arm as I flipped through more papers looking for anything that might have given some sort of end-of-life plan for this stranger, this man I didn't know outside of a few conversations Tristan had described him in. Nothing turned up. No instructions, no plans, nothing to indicate he was prepared to die in any way at all. There was no lifeline Tristan could cling to to know he was making the right choices for the end of his dad's life. There was nothing.

When I went back into the living room, Tristan was in the same place. He hadn't moved. He was staring at the spot his father had been, now empty as the body made its way to the morgue, then...where? I wasn't sure. Tristan would have to decide what needed to happen then, because as it stood, nothing was left behind to make the decision obvious.

I sat beside him and draped my arm over him, leaning into him and kissing his shoulder as I put the leather-bound book in his hand. "What's this?" he asked.

"It was on your dad's desk. I think you need to read it sometime," I told him. He held the notebook but didn't open it. Instead, he just kept staring.

Chapter Twenty-Three

I don't know if we sat there for another hour or another three hours. After a little bit, it was hard to discern the passage of time. Once the sun went down, I couldn't even use afternoon light to really figure it out. My back was giving out, pain screaming from my muscles and spine from the way I sat there, leaning against nothing to support me, my arms cradling Tristan while he stared into space. He didn't move, didn't speak, didn't flinch. A part of me is still absolutely certain he forgot I was there at all until I nodded off, my head slipping off his shoulder as I jerked awake again.

"You're tired," he said.

"I'm okay," I assured him. I rubbed his lower back gently.

"I'm tired," he added, as if to make me feel better about dozing off beside him.

I kissed his shoulder. "You want to go to my place tonight? I'm sure Alex will understand." I didn't know that staying there and him staring at the scene any longer would help things. There wasn't even anything to look at. His dad wasn't there, so why were we? I wasn't sure.

He shook his head. "I think I want to stay here tonight."

"Okay," I said. I tried to stifle a yawn. I was exhausted. I was pretty sure midnight had passed by then, but I didn't want him to know how drowsy I was because

I was worried that he'd feel bad. I was the last thing he needed to be concerned about that day. "Do you want me to come back to get you tomorrow, take you to the pool? I can," I offered. I started to untangle from him to stretch.

"Please stay," he asked softly, his voice barely above a whisper like he wasn't sure if he wanted me to hear him or not. I nodded and curled up in him again.

"As long as you need me," I promised. "Do you want to move to the couch?" Anything had to be better than sitting on brick for another second. My body couldn't handle more.

"We can sleep in my room if you want," he said. "It's only a full, but we can make it work probably," he told me. I had a double, and I didn't want to correct him then and tell him that doubles and fulls were the same size. Apparently, he hadn't noticed after being in my bed. He didn't need to worry. As he led me to his room, I realized I had to pretend this was the first time I'd seen it, to act like I hadn't stood there and stared before. Even if he thought I might have opened the door, he probably assumed I'd have closed it right away to find the office, so the drawings, he'd probably thought I'd never seen.

"Do you want me to wait here a minute?" I asked him. It was my chance to give him an out, to let him go back and situate the room, to take down the drawings if he wanted to, but I didn't want to tell him that. It would have outed the fact I'd looked once already.

"Why?" he asked me.

"I don't know. I just wasn't sure if you needed a minute."

"No," he said, standing up and taking my hand. "Come on." I followed him, and when he turned on the light, I saw his room for the second time. "Anyway, it's nothing special. Bed. Desk." He shrugged. I looked around, pretended like I was taking it in.

"It's nice," I said.

"Gets the job done." He glanced over at the sketches but didn't acknowledge them, sitting down on the bed. I sat beside him. "I might take a shower," he said. "If you want you can do whatever. I'm sorry I don't have a TV in here, but if you want to use the one in the front room, you can."

"It's okay," I said. "I'll probably just lay down for a little bit." He nodded to that and stripped his shirt off over his head and tossed it in the laundry pile. I tried to get comfortable on the bed, but the whole situation threw me for a loop. We were sleeping in his house for the first time ever, hours after we'd found his dad dead in that same house. It was hard not to feel a little weird about it, to wish I'd somehow successfully convinced him to go back to my place after all. Not because I didn't want to be here, but because there was something weird about sitting there alone with my thoughts in such a strange situation.

His shower felt like it took too long. Ten minutes felt okay. Twenty felt like it was stretching it and I started to worry. I crept down the hall, heard the shower water running, and I knocked and peeked my head in. "Tris? You okay?"

"Come here," he said weakly. I stepped forward, toward the shower.

"I'm here."

"No, I mean...will you come here? Like in here? With me?" he asked.

I nodded, but then I realized he couldn't hear me on the other side of the plain gray curtain. "Let me take my clothes off, okay?"

"'Kay," he answered. Silence followed, nothing but the sound of water flowing. I stepped in on the opposite side of the shower head, over the tub side and into the shower with him. He was facing the showerhead, letting it pour on him, and he had his face in his hands. I didn't say anything then. I didn't need to. Instead, I hooked my arms under his, wrapping them up and holding him at the shoulders, drawing his back to my chest and pressing my body against his to ground him.

"I'm here, Tris. I'm not going anywhere." For a few minutes, we stayed like that, me holding him from behind. After that, he turned and buried his face in the crook of my neck. His body shook with tears, a final release after holding it in all afternoon and evening. I knew tears would come eventually but knowing he would cry didn't make the fact it was happening any less alarming. I hated that there wasn't anything I could do or say to fix things, to make it right, to make him feel okay. Instead, I held him, arms around him to pull him close. His fingers pressed into my back painfully hard as he tried to get me closer. I couldn't get any closer without fusing our bodies together, becoming one with him in new ways. We were as close as we could get. I'm not even sure a droplet of water could squeeze between our bodies. My fingers played with his soaked hair, rubbing the back of his head like it would somehow fix everything. He cried. He cried until the water ran cold ten minutes later, and he cried until we both shivered.

"I'm going to turn the water off," I told him. "I don't think you should get hypothermia." He nodded barely, and I let go with one arm enough to turn the knobs to get the water off. We still didn't leave the shower, not for a while. We stayed there like that until my skin started to get dried off on its own.

"He's gone," he said quietly. I nodded.

"I'm sorry. I'm really, really sorry," I told him. I didn't know what else to say.

"I should have been here."

"You couldn't have saved him."

"I could have been here though." He didn't want his dad to go through it alone, and I understood that, even if I didn't think it would have helped him at all. Hell, it might have made it even worse.

"He kicked you out, Tris. You couldn't have," I reminded him.

"I should have checked in more. I should have known when he didn't read my texts. I thought he was just extra angry this time," he confessed. I didn't know he'd even been trying to get in touch with his dad. I felt bad for not asking, for not realizing. I figured he'd just blown it off. If I had known he was trying, getting ignored, I could have encouraged him to come home sooner. In fairness, with as much as I disliked his dad based on the information I had, I probably wouldn't have encouraged him to come home. I probably would have only made him hate me if he eventually did and thought I had kept him from his dad then. In a sick, selfish way, it was better how it happened if only because Tris didn't hate me.

"You did everything you could. There's nothing that would have changed this. Even if you'd have been here, Tristan. Even if. It might not have changed anything, okay?"

He nodded, but I don't think he believed me at all. Eventually, I stopped holding him just long enough so I could get us towels we didn't need. We'd already air dried but something felt wrong about walking naked through his family home, even if we knew it was just us. As I fell asleep that night, I realized he still hadn't read his father's journal.

Chapter Twenty-Four

I woke up an hour too late for class, but I hadn't even considered going anyway. I knew I was going to blow it off. I was able to skip class up to four times that summer, and I'd only missed it once, so I didn't think much of it. They could do without me for a day, but Tristan couldn't. When I woke, he was already awake, sitting at his desk sketching something. I wasn't sure what. I crawled out of bed, dressed only in my underwear, and I walked over to him, wrapped my arms around him, and kissed his bare shoulder. He hadn't bothered to get dressed, either, a throw draped over his lap. The sketch was a hand again, but this wasn't ours. It was his dad's, I was sure. It had a fly on the finger, and it made me want to throw up. On the rest of the page, there were other hands drawn, all his dad's. In the top corner was the open leather-bound book, held in one hand as the other hand penned words into it. In the bottom corner was his dad's hand wrapped around a glass, half-empty of ice and whiskey. It was like a study, a few detailed bits leading up to the center drawing, the fly, the focus of what was on his mind. I could tell he wasn't doing well. He didn't move when I kissed his shoulder, not the first time or the second time. He just kept drawing.

"You want me to run and get breakfast for us?" I asked him. My words snapped him out of his daze. My touch hadn't gotten his attention, but speaking led him to jump, like it was the first time he'd even noticed me next to him, behind him.

"You don't have to," he told me. But I did have to. I had to get out of that house, if only for ten minutes. I'd come right back, sure. I'd be there with him every step of the way. But right then, I had to get out of the house. I needed air, air that I didn't feel was tinged with death. There was still a stain in his dad's chair from where he'd been, and I couldn't get it out of my head. I couldn't stop smelling his dad no matter how many candles I lit or how I held my breath.

"Okay," he told me. When I asked what he wanted, I was met with a shrug. My bubbly, bright, overenthusiastic Tristan was missing. He'd been replaced with a quiet, near-robotic boy so focused on his sketch he barely noticed anything around him. I'd watched him sketch before, and he was always more aware than this. Today, he was a shell of himself. He seemed hollow.

On the drive back from getting breakfast, I dreaded walking inside. I realized there was a hope inside me that when I got back in, Tristan would have snapped back to his old self, greeted me with a kiss, moved from his desk, something. Instead, I knocked and immediately turned the knob. I was optimistic but I wasn't stupid. I knew Tristan wasn't going to let me in. The phone was ringing. "Tristan!" I yelled, hands full of a bag of food and a drink tray carrying coffees. "Tris? Phone!" I yelled again. Nothing. I scrambled to the kitchen counter, set the food and drinks down, and answered. "Um," I said, hesitating, "McCarthy residence. Can I take a message?"

I was terrified it would be someone calling for his dad, a call I'd have to somehow navigate and either explain that he was deceased or pass to Tristan and let him cover it. I didn't know what I'd do in that situation. Instead, it was the coroner, asking where we wanted Tristan's dad transported. I had no idea.

"Tris?" I called. No answer. "Can I have him call you back in a couple of hours? I'm really not sure what he's looking at doing just yet, and we're still trying to find out if his dad had any sort of end of life plans figured out," I explained.

"May I ask who I'm speaking to?" the voice on the other end asked me. I didn't know what to tell her. I had no idea. What were we?

"I'm, um..." I wasn't his boyfriend. I was...I was what? I couldn't tell her we were friends with benefits or fuck buddies. That would have been weird. And to be honest, I felt like we were so much more than that. Friend didn't cover it.

"My partner," a voice crackled through on another phone. "I'll call you back later. I'm still sorting through things. Thanks for taking care of him." I heard Tristan's phone click. I hadn't even realized he'd been on the line at all.

"I'll call back," she said, I guess still assuming I was on the line. I thanked her and hung up the phone. I didn't ask Tristan about what he'd said. Not then, not ever. There wasn't a good time, and by the time he was himself again, it wasn't worth us discussing. What he'd said existed in that moment and that moment alone. It was the easiest way to explain what we were in a moment where nothing made sense.

"I'm sorry for answering the phone," I told him when I took the bag of food back to him and put the coffee on his desk next to his charcoal-smudged hand. "I wasn't trying to overstep. I just thought the call might be important. I didn't know you'd gotten it." He put his hand on mine, which was still on the cup, and for the first time since we'd gotten there, he *really* looked me in the eyes.

"Connor, don't. Thank you. I was going to answer, but...I don't know. I wasn't sure what to say." He looked down again and I could see the tears welling in his eyes, threatening to spill over again, just like the rain had been doing for two days consistently.

"Eat something," I encouraged him, opening the bag and passing him an egg sandwich. "Then talk to me. Or don't. Whatever you want to do." I was okay with whatever felt right to him, honestly. I didn't have a choice but to be okay with that. He put the sandwich in his lap and looked at me again, this time with determination in his eyes.

"We should go somewhere today."

"Where?" I asked him.

"I haven't figured that part out yet."

Chapter Twenty-Five

I forgot all about my shift at the pool. I don't know how, because I'd worked there every day but the few Greg gave me off, and somehow, I'd still forgotten it altogether until we were pulling into the parking lot of the amusement park. The day didn't feel amusing, the situation didn't, but perhaps the juxtaposition of our inner pain with the joy that parks like this brought would be cathartic in some way. Regardless, my phone buzzed in the parking lot with a call from Greg. I was an hour and a half away from the pool and there was no way for me to get there in time. "I'm so sorry," I told him. "I can't believe I didn't think about my shift. I...I had a family emergency and—"

I was met with annoyance, his snap telling me he didn't believe it. "What kind of family emergency? Do you have some sort of proof you'll be able to bring in?" People claimed family emergencies all the time and they didn't have one. It was an easy way off work.

"There was a death in the family," I explained. Tristan wasn't exactly family, and I'd never met his dad, but what other way could I explain the fact I wasn't coming into work today? Tristan didn't so much as glance at me to confirm or deny if what I'd just said was okay. That seemed to calm Greg down, my answer, to make him more sympathetic. When he asked who, I repeated Tristan's words. "My partner's dad. I guess I got distracted with arrangements." Tristan reached for my arm and tugged it toward himself gently to hold my hand. He brought my knuckles to his lips and kissed them. "Yeah, okay. Monday sounds good." Three days. Greg gave me three days to get in a better frame of mind, a better place. It wasn't so much about Tristan's dad impacting me as it was about Tristan's loss, the way he was responding to it.

When I hung up, Tristan didn't ask me about my wording in the same way I hadn't asked him about his. Right now, they were necessary words, words we'd unsay later, words that would find their natural conclusion when they did. There was no way to explain to the outside world what we were because we didn't know ourselves. We were young and we were tangled in each other in ways we couldn't separate ourselves, knotted together in ways that had yet to unravel, so for those few days, it was easiest to pick a word, to tell the people who needed to hear it, and to keep going as we were, not speaking it to each other, not saying anything outside of our normal conversations. As normal as they could be, at least, despite everything. We defined our relationship for others in ways we couldn't define it for ourselves, in ways we wouldn't, and that was okay.

"Where are we going?" I asked Tristan as I followed him through the park. We didn't have a map, and we didn't need one. We had the day. We had time, and I'd have followed him anywhere in the park no matter where he led me. I was there for him, for the sheer fact this was where he wanted to be. But he had a place in mind, one specific thing he seemed driven toward. I was not a roller coaster kind of person, not even remotely. Risk wasn't in my vocabulary, and that wasn't anything new. I think Tristan realized that in the stark pale sickness of my face once we arrived at his chosen coaster, something wooden and tall.

"We don't have to," he said. "I mean, there are other things we could do." For a moment, I almost took the out he was giving me and suggested corn dogs instead. But I shook my head and held his hand tighter.

"Let's do it. I'm in." Better to do it then, before the corn dog, than to change my mind and try to do it after we ate. I'd brave it, risk it, face my crippling fear of heights. Anything to see him smile, to have *my* Tristan back. He hadn't smiled since we got burgers, and as I thought back, I realized he hadn't been smiling much then either. It had been too long, the longest I'd seen him go without a flash of the lopsided smiles he always gave me, the ones that made me happiest. I needed to see that happiness again. We were strapped in side by side and I gripped his hand until my knuckles were white.

"Easy," he said. "You might break me." It was meant to be a joke, and the turned-up corner of his lips made that obvious, but there was still a sadness to his tone, more to do with his dad than the words he'd said, and they hit home too hard. I might break him. He might break me. We might break each other. But then he squeezed my hand tighter, too, and neither of us let go.

I don't know which of us screamed louder at the drop. Me, out of sheer terror, or him, out of a need to get everything out. Either way, the sound reverberated in my ears, blood curdling. We rode the coaster twice more, waiting in line, screaming, free falling. I didn't love it the first time or the third time, but the journey wasn't about that. It was about feeling. Or perhaps not feeling. It was about anything but thinking, and when we were falling, when we were propelled forward far too fast, I wasn't thinking. I wasn't thinking when Tristan pulled me toward the roller coaster exit. I wasn't thinking when he pressed me against a wall and kissed me hard. I wasn't thinking when we bought the biggest cotton candy we could find and split it and tasted the sugar crystalized on each other's lips. I'd have to think later. I'd have to think when we got back to his house. But when we were at the park? I didn't think, not from the first moment we got onto that roller coaster. I couldn't think.

We rode almost all the coasters, skipping water rides altogether. We hadn't thought to bring bathing suits, but there were plenty of roller coasters I didn't want to ride for us to check out and go on. Halfway through, I whined half-heartedly that my legs were tired from walking. He wanted to ride one more coaster on the other side of the park, promising it would be the last one and then we could do something milder. Tristan's solution was to hoist me onto his back, piggybacking me through the park, my arms around his neck and legs wrapping his waist. I couldn't resist planting small kisses on his neck.

"You should stop that, or I won't be able to resist fucking you here in the middle of this park," he told me. It was the flirtiest he'd been since...well, since anything had happened. The park had an almost magical transformation on us. For that afternoon, we were us before instead of us after, and he flirted with me openly.

"In that case," I mumbled, kissing his neck again, licking the shell of his ear with a small giggle.

"That's it," he sighed, putting me down in a grassy patch near a walkway. I laid down and he laid next to me, holding my hand and looking at the clouds. That was the thing about amusement parks: there was never enough shade. It didn't matter though. We had clouds to watch, soft kisses to exchange. People walked past but we didn't care. He held my hand and I pointed out a cloud shaped like an elephant. Somehow, he was convinced it was a hot air balloon shape instead. We bickered quietly about what the cloud looked like until he shut me up with another kiss.

"Should we find that ride?" I asked him.

"In a minute," he told me. "Not yet. We have time. We have so much time." He was trying hard to convince himself, I knew. Neither of us had time, slapped in the face with mortality. Not the kind of mortality like his dad faced, even though we both knew we'd all end up that way in the end. The kind of mortality that meant the death of summer, the death of this, the death of whatever we had. We were running out of time and we knew it. My hand was on his cheek and I pulled him closer.

"We do," I told him. The roller coaster was the last thing we did for the day, because after we got off it, the clouds were no longer light and fluffy, good for watching. Instead, they were dark and menacing, with lightning shutting the rides down. We got one more cotton candy for the road, and he fed it to me as I drove. The closer we got to his house, the less it felt like we had the time he'd promised me, the time I'd agreed to. His mood shifted from bubbly pink to dark-gray, from cotton candy to ash.

"Don't leave me alone tonight," he said when I pulled into the driveway. I had no plans to.

Chapter Twenty-Six

That night he cried when he was inside me. It wasn't about the whole sex part. It was the feelings of everything, the comedown after the surge of emotions, the release after the ache. Like a roller coaster, we'd been at the peak, and now we were at the depths. Hell, we were nearly underground. I would have cried, too, if I didn't feel some desperate need to hold it together, to be the stable one in that moment, to be the one who wasn't drowning in the ache of loss. It wasn't my loss to feel pain over, but a part of me still felt it intensely anyway, the weight of the pain evident in the teardrops landing like dew on my skin. "I'm sorry," he said, swiping one of his own tears from my cheek. I shook my head and pulled him closer, kissing him and tugging his lower lip between my teeth. I could feel his moan more than I could hear it.

The sex that night was healing. It was hurting. It was something. I couldn't be sure what it was. "Roll over," he encouraged, and I did what he asked. Instead of his usual soft kisses to my back, I could feel his teeth pressing against my skin, and his hands gripped me tighter. He was hurting and I was hurting, and I needed more. I needed more of anything he needed to get out of him in that moment.

"Bite me," I groaned, and he did, his teeth grazing at my flesh, my shoulder bearing the indentations of each one. He pulled me back onto him harder and faster, pushing into me, against me, the sound of our skin slapping against each other in his bed in his childhood room, sketches of us together on the walls. He gripped the sections of my hair that were long enough to hold and tugged my head backward to pull me in for a kiss. I sat up enough to give him that, to kiss him, arching my back and doing whatever it took to reach him the way he wanted me. I needed him, craved him, had to have him, and he kept going until I could feel him filling me.

I didn't need release, not then. Even if he offered it, I didn't want it. I needed to hold him, to let him hold me, to let his body cover mine again until he was feeling okay. I needed that way more than I needed to finish. When he tried to get his hands on me, to coax me over the edge, I brushed him off. "Hold me," I pleaded, and he did until I turned over and wrapped my arms around him instead, kissing his chest and cradling him against me until I could feel soft, sleepy breaths against my skin.

I didn't go home. For days on end, I was there with Tristan. Alex texted me and asked if I'd be back soon, but I ignored the messages. I ignored everything in the world but Tristan until Sunday. The weekend was a blur as Tristan made arrangements, deciding he wanted his dad cremated for lack of any better options. His dad didn't have friends or family for any real funeral, so we drove over and said a quiet goodbye. I let Tristan have time alone with him. That felt like the right thing to do, to give him time to say goodbye. After, I held his hand and stood there with him.

On Saturday, he paid overdue bills to avoid the lights being shut off, and he tried piecing together the remnants of his life, trying to sift through things his dad left behind. Emotionally, he still wasn't there. He'd start showers alone and finish them calling for me, letting me hold him and wash him because he couldn't do it himself.

On Sunday morning, I woke up to Tristan sitting at his desk again. This time, he wasn't sketching. Instead, he held the journal in his hands. His body shook. "Morning," I mumbled, trying to wake up.

"Why didn't you tell me?" he asked.

"Tell you what?" I was half asleep still, too tired to know what he was talking about really.

"Why didn't you tell me he loved me?" he asked me, sobbing as I stood and wrapped my arms around him. He sank to the floor and I sat on the edge of the bed, his head in my lap as I ran my fingers down his shoulders and back.

"I thought you needed to read it," I told him. It wasn't my place to tell him what the journal said. For all I knew, it would have only made things worse if I'd told him instead of letting him wait to read it until he was truly ready.

"I thought he hated me," he said, words broken through sobs. "I thought I was a burden to him."

"I don't think he thought that, Tris. I think he was hurting really badly. I think it was a lot for him to process, and I think it hurt, but I think he always loved you," I promised him. I'd think anyone would have to love their child deeply if they continued to raise them, knowing everything was a lie, even if his dad made a whole hell of a lot of mistakes. Even if I was still angry with a dead man for the ways he'd hurt someone I cared so much for, someone I...loved...I knew he had to love Tristan. My nails gently scratched Tris's scalp, massaging it softly. It took us half an hour of silence and sobs before Tristan calmed down enough to get up from the floor and sit down next to me. He leaned his head on my shoulder and I wrapped an arm around him.

We were quiet for a long time, and when he calmed down, he moved to the desk chair and pulled me into his lap. He kissed me, whispered to me. "I need you. I have to feel you, Connor." No pet name. No pretty boy or babe or honey. Just my name, my name and his need to feel okay, to feel like it would be all right. I rode him like that, his arms wrapped tightly around my body, me in his lap, grinding down on him as he kissed me, his hands holding me in place, holding me tighter than he needed to, like if he let go, I might float away. I wasn't going anywhere, though. I was there, tethered to him by the way he was inside me, the way he was kissing me, hell, the way he looked at me. I was there. I was present and in our contact for as long as I could be. He had me, all the way, in every way.

That day, Sunday, marked two weeks before the end of summer, two weeks before life would go back to so-called normal. Sunday was the day Tristan decided to enroll in an art program, accepting their offer late. It was the day any dream of me having more than the summer with him was shattered. Two weeks. Two weeks and it would all be over. Two weeks and he'd be a thousand miles away. It was my own stupid fault. I'd been encouraging him to follow his dream every step of the way.

Chapter Twenty-Seven

"Do you think your roommate will mind if I stay over?" Tristan asked on Sunday evening. "I have to get out of here. I'm going crazy in this house." He was restless, jittery in a way I hadn't seen him before. I didn't blame him. I didn't want to stay there another second, either.

"Yeah, I mean...it's okay. You can come over," I told him. I didn't know if Alex would be cool about it or not if I was being honest. It didn't matter though. If Tristan couldn't stay in the house, I wasn't about to make him. I'd fight Alex if I had to.

"I couldn't get it out of my head, you know? I mean I know we had to stay so I could deal with the phone calls and stuff, but I really need out of here," he told me. I nodded and waited as he packed a bag. I was wearing his shirt, and I forgot to look for my own shirt in his laundry pile on the floor. I never did get it back from him, but then, I never tried to. I still have his shirt, too, and I wear it sometimes when it's been a while since I last wore it, and I think of him. I don't wash the shirt much. Maybe that's gross. Maybe it's also necessary.

"I know," I said. I wrapped my arms around him and kissed his shoulder. "Come on. Let's go home." I don't know why I called it home, other than it was my home, but he followed anyway, bag slung over his shoulder.

I think it was unspoken, the way we both knew time was running out, ticking away the second he made his choice, the one that would take him to a school he was better suited for. We tried not to talk about it or think about it, to give words to the knowledge that in two weeks, our summer would be over. Instead, I drove him home and we listened to music like it was any other day, any other drive. On the way back, we got Slurpees, just like always. That day, our kisses were green and slightly yellow, even if it's hard to turn a tongue yellow with a drink. Close enough. He tasted like bananas, not real ones, but that fakey flavored kind. I felt like I was hyperaware of that sort of thing then, how he smelled and how he tasted, the way he looked at me. I was trying to memorize all of it before it was too late.

That night, his hands were on me and we made love again, but this was different. It no longer had the hatred of early summer or the lust that followed. It didn't have the tearful despair of everything we did at his house. This was different. This was desperate, passionate, intense. The word "fucking" still didn't apply here. What we did was too much for that. For the first time, Tristan was the one moving things along, trying to rush them forward. I was wanting to savor every second, to slow him down, to beg him closer. He trailed his lips down my body, sucking me off faster than usual, flashing his eyes up to mine and working me harder. When I thought I might explode, he stopped, mostly to make me wait, kissing my thighs and moving my leg until my knee was at my chest. He kissed my foot, rubbing it with his hands like he wanted to give me a massage. His lips trailed to my ankle and his hands roamed up my legs. He'd gone from racing to a dead halt, not touching me where I desperately needed release at all, instead touching every other part of me. I could have waited forever. This time, I didn't beg him to get me off, didn't plead with him to fuck me. I let him do that for a minute or two, far less time than I expected he'd spend on it, because then he was covering me, his body draped on mine again, his lips on my neck. "I'm going to make you come so hard," he promised me, "you're never going to forget it." It was intense, and I'm not sure he meant it that way. I think he was trying to tease, trying to bring a sense of lightheartedness we hadn't had since before we'd gone to his house, but instead it came out differently, like a reminder of how little time we had to capture moments to remember each other in. The words were like a knife in my heart, but somehow still a welcome one.

"I'm not going to forget," I promised him. He needed the reassurance as much as I did. He pushed into me and he was right—I didn't take long to come at all, and I still haven't forgotten how he felt. It's the kind of feeling you take to your grave, the kind of eye contact that burns in your memory, the kind you pull out to think of when you're alone and it's late and you miss someone desperately. It's that sort of feeling, and it still sticks with me. Ten, fifteen years from now it'll probably still stick with me.

The next day, I had to go back to work. I didn't want to. I wanted to stay in bed with Tristan, to spend our last two weeks in my room with his body on me, in me, over me. I couldn't. School was necessary; work was necessary. He didn't come with me. Instead, I dropped him off at his house on my way to class. "You going to the pool today?" I asked him. He shook his head.

"I have to start packing," he told me. He was contacting a realtor. If he was leaving for school, there was no sense in trying to hold on to the property. He didn't have the money to pay the bills anyway, not if he was also trying to manage his life somewhere else. He leaned into the driver's side window, kissed me, and promised me he'd help me with my paper that night if I'd pick him up after my shift. I said I would. He excelled at every subject I sucked at. Sometimes it seemed like he was a natural at everything he did.

"Where's Tristan?" James demanded when he saw me. I shrugged.

"I don't know." It was a lie, but I didn't want to explain everything we'd been through that weekend.

"Bullshit," James told me. "You go away for days, skip a bunch of shifts, he's not here at all, and now you're back and he's not? What'd you do to him?" His tone was accusatory and angry.

"Nothing," I said. James rolled his eyes.

"Listen, I don't know how you went from hating him to fucking him or whatever, but at least have the decency not to lie to me. Did he stop coming because of what happened? Because I really need to know." For the first time, I saw the insecurity in James that Tristan saw. Instead of the "he has to fuck me" cocky little attitude I'd seen, there was a boy, terrified he'd made someone leave altogether.

"He's not dodging you," I said. "You ever heard of Carly Simon?" I got the insecurity, but the shit Tristan was going through was way bigger than what James had done.

"What do you mean?" he asked.

"Nothing," I said. There was no explaining to James he was vain enough to think Tristan thought enough of him to leave the pool because of him. I knew for a fact that Tristan had moved on from what happened, mostly because it was so insignificant compared to the things we were facing now. Even if it wasn't, Tristan wasn't the kind of guy who would avoid the pool over a few shitty remarks on James's part. "He's not avoiding you," I promised again. "He had some shit happen, and I think he's going to be pretty busy for a while."

"He going to be back before summer's over?" James asked. Deep down, a part of him, the part with the crush he'd had all summer, still wanted to see Tristan, even if he didn't have a shot in hell at him. I wish I could say I couldn't relate, but I remembered how I felt back in the beginning, back when Tristan had been gone for a little bit when his dad kicked him out. I related hard, and I felt bad for James.

"I have no idea," I said. I hoped so, because working without Tristan there was boring. I hated admitting that to myself. Even though things had changed, and I was in over my head with how into Tristan I was, I hated admitting to the fact that yeah, I liked work better when he was being ridiculous. He'd calmed down anyway, most of the way, after he'd gotten my attention. He'd still been splashing me during lifeguard swim, but now I read it as flirty instead of annoying, and it bugged me when he wasn't there. For lifeguard swim now, I swam laps. I figured I may as well get back into shape before fall, to actually swim. It wasn't my preference, but with Tristan not there to give me an excuse to do something else, why not?

There was one advantage I had over James though. Tristan may not have been at the pool to make work better, but as soon as I was off work, Tristan was all mine. In those lazy, quiet moments after work, I got him all to myself. I was clinging to that as I swam laps, my body cutting through the water, wearing myself out because I was so out of shape. As I heaved myself up on the side of the pool, I huffed and puffed. I had fifteen minutes of lifeguard swim. I only swam for seven. The last thing I wanted was to be too tired to let Tristan have me when we had so little time left.

Chapter Twenty-Eight

Alex asked exactly once why Tristan was doing the same thing over again, staying over instead of going home. Tristan was in the shower that morning, one of the few mornings I didn't really have time to join him. I was slamming through a bowl of cereal, trying to eat quickly before I had to leave for class. "Is he ever leaving?" Alex phrased it, and I wanted to slap him and say "yeah, he's leaving way too soon." But I also understood where Alex was coming from. He'd been more than patient with us. Still, I didn't want to think about Tristan leaving.

Instead, I told Alex he didn't want to be at home every night. "His dad just died, man. Would you want to be alone in that creepy-ass house?" I asked.

"No. I just don't get why y'all aren't staying over there together, then," he said, but his tone was a little more compassionate by that point.

"He's there all day by himself trying to pack everything and clean. If he wants to sell it before he leaves, he may not even *have* a place to stay," I told him. "He's not bugging you. What's wrong with him staying for a few more days?" It was true. When Tristan was there, he was pretty much always in my room. The only thing that would have affected Alex at all was the sound of us fucking, which admittedly had to be annoying but it was something we would've done whether or not Tristan slept over, and the fact the shower had one more person using it. The thing was, Tristan showered at a different time than either of us, so even that didn't impact him much.

"Fine. Whatever." Alex shrugged. "What's he going to do when he sells the house? He can't live here this fall," he told me.

"He's leaving," I promised. "He won't be here but what, another week?" Saying the words aloud hurt like hell. One more week and Tristan was gone, and my head was doing that mental count.

With seven days left, Tristan was almost done packing. He'd stuck almost everything in storage that was worth saving, packed the little he needed to keep in a suitcase he kept in the corner of my room. I hated that suitcase because it was a constant reminder this wasn't permanent. Some of his sketches he'd taped on my wall instead, mostly at my request that he do it because my walls were boring, and I didn't want them getting torn up in his bag. He picked his favorites, taping them up above the bed, and I fell asleep looking up at them with his head on my shoulder. Almost every day, without any real warning or without him saying anything, he'd add a new one. That day, it was a sketch with pastels added, our tongues the only colorful thing in the picture, a memory of what had now become near-daily Slurpee runs and lazy make outs after. In the picture, his tongue was blue and mine was vivid red—unnaturally so compared to the normal pinkness of it.

When we had six days left, Tristan laid on my bed, and I laid on the floor. I traced out bold block letters reading YARD SALE with arrows pointing toward his house from wherever we might leave the signs. He filled in my traced letters with thick black marker, getting smudges on the side of his hands that would stay there until the day before he left. That night he used his marker-smudged hands to pull my body down onto him, gripping my waist and clinging to me as he cried out into my shoulder, coming hard as I spilled onto the bed under us. We didn't bother to change the sheets before falling asleep. That night he slept halfway on top of me, both of us naked, the top sheet somewhere near our ankles, the fan on the dresser raising goose bumps on my skin with each oscillation.

When six days became five days, we woke up two hours before my class to stake the signs around the streets leading to his house and then hauled every piece of furniture and clothing that he was selling out of the door. We were almost done when I had to leave, and I debated missing class to help him, but he shook his head, pulled me in for a kiss, and told me he'd see me after. That night, he was exhausted, and he sketched while I poured oil on his back, rubbing it into his muscles and kneading it with my knuckles, hearing his spine pop and listening to him groan in pleasure. Every once in a while, he'd say "ouch," and I'd freeze, but then he'd say "keep going. It's a good hurt." That was a good way to sum up how I felt about only having a few days left with him—it was a good hurt. The sketch he added that day was the picture he had from the mirror he'd put in front of himself while I rubbed his back: me straddling him, hands working his body slowly, making sure I'd covered every inch. That sketch wasn't finished, mostly because he'd abandoned trying when I asked him to roll over. I rubbed his arms and legs, taking things as slowly as he always liked to, and then working my way back up to the main focus. As I tugged him off gently with my hands, I took my time, talking him through it and telling him how good he looked like that. It wasn't until he was thrusting up into my hands, balling the sheets up in his fists as he squirmed and writhed for more, that I sped up, helping him finish fast and all over both of us. I wiped us off with a towel beside the bed and forgot to wash it until after he'd been gone for days.

Four days before he had to leave, I had a nightmare. I jolted awake, startled in the night, and worried I'd wake him with my erratic breathing. I didn't, thankfully, and he slept soundly. I made my way under his arm, and in his sleep, he pulled me closer to him. I dreaded how, in a few short days, if I had a nightmare, he wouldn't be there to hold me, even if he didn't realize that's what had happened at all. That day at the pool, I couldn't get the thought out of my head, the idea that he'd be gone soon, and I'd be incredibly screwed. I was tired, barely sleeping because sleep meant time wasted when I could have been with him. Greg tossed an audit ball into my section that day. I had thought audits were over—summer almost was, so what was the point of continuing to test us?—but they weren't, and I didn't see it at all. He called me into his office, told me he was disappointed, that I'd done good work all summer and he hated seeing me slip up so close to the end. I promised I wouldn't let it happen again, and he nodded, telling me I needed to go deal with whatever my head was distracted with and come back the next day. It was standard practice, sending someone home when they missed an audit, leaving half a day's work unpaid as punishment for not paying attention. The problem was my brain wouldn't be clear, not that day, not the rest of the summer. I didn't know how to tell Greg that, to tell him if he expected me to pay attention to the audits, then he may as well fire me, because I was hopeless at the end of summer, at least this time around. It was funny to me how annoyed I'd been at the beginning of summer anytime someone would miss a ball. I wondered how they could be so stupid, so blind not to see it, and I wondered what was wrong with their head that they'd let something representing a person basically drown. Now, I was just lucky it was an audit ball and not an actual life, because I was on track to go from the best lifeguard to the worst one. If I wanted to come back to the pool, I might have worked harder, but it wasn't like I was aiming for head lifeguard.

That day, I headed from the pool straight to Tristan's to help him finish up the yard sale he was having. That night he signed papers with a realtor. Someone who had stopped by asked about the reason for the yard sale, took a peek, and loved the house, said it would be a nice project to flip. They put in an offer immediately, just below the asking price Tristan had set. He was tired, he was sad, and he wasn't in the mood to let the house sit. There were days left before he had to board a plane, and even though I offered to work with the realtor for him, I think he was done caring about it. The house held so many memories, good and bad, and I think he felt the need to be away from them, so I didn't argue with him when he said he was selling it. That night, we cleaned up the last of the stuff, dragging it to the road and taping a sign on it reading FREE in large letters. I took him home. "I can't believe it's gone now," he told me.

"We still have time to stop the deal if you changed your mind," I said, rubbing my hand down his back as he sat on my bed.

"No. I don't want to," he said. I understood. It had been a long summer, a long past few days, and he was tired. The sketch he did that day didn't hang on the wall. It stayed in his bag. It was the only sketch I'd ever seen him do that wasn't about people in some way. Instead, it was a drawing of the house, down to the tiny brick detailing.

When there were three days left until he had to go, I asked if he wanted to go to the pool with me. He didn't have a yard sale, packing, a house to worry about so I figured maybe he'd want something to do. He shook his head. "I think I'm going to take a walk, if it's okay. And then I think I might sleep." I nodded. It wasn't like him to choose sleep. Usually he liked the pool, and opting for sleep over anything else? The Tristan I met at the beginning of summer wasn't that person, and it hurt to see him hurt. I could tell he was aching, too, but I didn't know how to snap him out of it, and with work and school, I didn't know if I even had the time. That night, when he came back, he had flowers for me. They were bright-blue, unnatural like pool water. "These made me think of you," he told me.

"They're beautiful," I said. I smelled them, and they didn't really smell like anything, but they looked pretty anyway. I sat them on my dresser where the drawing of my dick had been before we'd hung it on the walls. He told me they were beautiful like me, and I wanted to cry. That night when I slept, he didn't, overly awake from the nap he'd taken all afternoon. Instead, he sketched me smelling the flowers. The desk light didn't wake me. I didn't move at all until morning.

The day before he had to leave, I thought about calling in sick and skipping class, but he woke me up with a kiss. "I edited your paper," he said, putting it on my chest, red marks covering it. He was struggling to sleep again, like the night before, and he'd spent it working on my paper instead of anything else. I wanted to cry.

"Thank you," I told him, and I kissed him back. I pinned him to the bed, tried to spark something, to thank him properly, but he tickled my ribs and I flinched off him.

"You have class," he reminded me. "But don't worry. Tonight, I am going to blow your mind."

"Oh yeah?"

"Oh yeah. I'm going to fuck your brains out, Connor. Gotta make sure you don't forget me." The last part stung. I could never forget him. We had something together, something beautiful, something I couldn't forget, sex or no sex.

"I'm never going to forget you," I said, but my tone was too solemn for the lighthearted way he'd intended it, and he kissed me again.

"That's mutual, pretty boy. Go on. Go to school. Do you want me to come with you and sit in the car, or do you want to swing by and pick me up for the pool after?" he asked, smacking my butt as he did and then watching me as I tugged my shorts on. For all the lighthearted ways he acted, there was still something different about him, still something that read a little off. Maybe it was the sleep deprivation, maybe it was the nerves about leaving, and maybe it was me seeing something that wasn't there. But things had changed and to me, it seemed like he was trying to be the Tristan I'd known, and instead he was a different Tristan. It wasn't bad, but it was like he hadn't quite figured out that he'd changed, and he was wearing the suit of his former self to cling to the beginning of everything.

I told him I could do whatever he wanted, drive him to class or come get him after. "I don't want to miss a minute," he said, getting dressed and following me to the car. We barely had any time left. It was like we were both too aware of the twenty-six hours that remained. After class, he kissed me and held my hand and then asked me if my paper needed any more revisions on his part as if we had all the time in the world for that sort of thing. Even if the assignment had needed more work from him, I wasn't about to ask. I wanted that time for me, to be selfish. Fuck the paper. I wanted his time. I wanted his attention.

Work was more awkward than anything. Tristan reconnected with friends he used to come to the pool with every day, and I realized very suddenly that he hadn't actually been talking to them. I wondered if it was my fault, the fact he'd ditched his friends. Then I worried it was about his dad. Instead, I realized something I hadn't known; they were only ever summer friends, people who connected because of a mutual location and then parted ways when the season ended. I'd always assumed they were so much closer than that, besties, but he'd cleared that up later when I asked. "They were just guys from the pool, Connor. Why would I have spent that time with them?" I shrugged. I'd never realized. At the pool, James avoided Tristan. He didn't avoid looking, but he avoided talking. Part of me wanted to tell James this would be his last chance to talk to him, to say goodbye or whatever, but I didn't. What was the point?

They had nothing outside of a few awkward conversations. Leave it to Tristan, though, to be the bigger person. At the end of my shift, he gave James a small wave. "Hey, have a good rest of your summer, man," he told him. "I have a feeling this fall is going to be a total game changer for you. Going back to school with a tan like that?" Tristan let out a low whistle and James's face lit up like he'd won some kind of contest. I was a little surprised how not-jealous I was over the exchange. I knew that was their last contact, but I had more time with Tristan. Not much, but more than James had.

As soon as we got out of earshot of James, Tristan leaned into me, sliding his hand down my back. "Remember what I told you this morning? I've got some big plans for you tonight, pretty boy."

Chapter Twenty-Nine

He wasn't joking. He had serious plans, and I wasn't ready for them. For every time that summer I thought Tristan had taken things slowly, taken his time with me, this was even more excruciating in the best ways. He lit candles. He rubbed my back and kissed down my spine, and when I figured he was going to do something, to fuck me, to anything, he didn't. He kept going slowly, teasing me until I worried that I wouldn't be able to take anymore. "You gonna fuck me?" I asked him, trying to goad him into it, and he laughed.

Leaning down close to my ear, he half-growled out the words "how many times do you think you can come for me tonight?"

I bit my lip and shook my head. "I don't know," I said.

"Guess we're going to find out, aren't we, Mister Impatient?" he said, putting his hands on me to flip me over. "We don't have to take it slow if you don't want to. This time." It was a promise and a threat, a clear indication that he was making the most of the last night we had together. Then, without any more preamble or hesitance, he fucked me. It was harder, faster, more intense than even the time he'd fucked me at the pool. He didn't go slow, didn't wait. No, he pounded me into the mattress until I was genuinely screaming over how good it was, coming all over myself and begging him not to stop.

He kept going until he was done, collapsing onto me, and kissing me—my lips, my neck, my collarbones.

"Fuck," I told him after, trying to catch my breath. I sucked in air until my ribs showed, doing what I could to compose myself after that. He laid down beside me, tracing my ribs with his fingertips.

"You've got a round two in you, right? I mean, not now but...you know. Soon." I nodded, still unable to catch my breath much. "Good. Because I'm not done with you Connor. You set on getting any sleep at all?"

I shook my head. "No sleep," I agreed. We could sleep later. I was already planning on using my last absence from class to take him to the airport, calling in sick to work to give him those last few minutes. I could nap the following day. That night, all that mattered was using every second I had with Tristan. He talked to me then, in the in between moments, after we fucked, before we fucked again.

"I'm sad," he said. No clarification, though, it seemed like he had plenty of reasons to be.

"Why?" I asked. It wasn't that I didn't think he should be. On the contrary. I simply didn't know what was most pressing then. He took my hand and traced over the lines of my palm with his fingers.

"I wish we had more time is all. I wish I didn't have to go."

It took everything in me not to tell him not to go, to tell him he could change his mind, stay with me, stay here, stay in this. I desperately wanted to say those words, but I knew they were all wrong. Keeping him wasn't fair to him, and it wasn't fair to what we had together. It was always supposed to end. Hell, it was never supposed to begin, but when it did, there was always an ending. We knew that. Changing the path now would have been wrong, making him stay because I couldn't be without him. I was sure what he was feeling, the idea he didn't want to go, was temporary. He'd get where he was going, and then eventually he'd move on. I knew that, and I didn't want to be the one keeping him stuck here. Not when he didn't have anything else keeping him; I didn't want him to stay for me.

"I do too," I settled on. It was close enough to "please stay" without me saying as much. The words were an acknowledgement that I didn't like this ending in the same way he didn't, but also an acknowledgement that I wasn't going to keep him from the life he deserved to live.

"Now that you're fucked out and you got to come, you're gonna let me take it slow this time, right?" he asked me. I nodded and smiled, letting him take his time. The smallest candles burned themselves out before we finished, their last dying embers sputtering out sometime when he had his lips on my shoulder and his fingers inside me, playing with me, stretching me, keeping me ready for everything he wanted.

Coming once didn't mean I wasn't insatiable. It was like my body knew just as well as my mind that he was leaving soon, and I had to get these moments in while I could. He flattened his body against mine again, covering me like he loved to do. We connected at all points as he kissed my neck. "You look so good, Connor," he told me. I reached behind my head to pull him in for another kiss.

"You do," I said. He slid into me the second time and I was pretty sure I couldn't breathe. Not in a bad way, either, but in the best way. He overwhelmed me. He made me feel different than I'd ever felt before. And all of that frustrated me because this was the end. I had no idea if I'd ever feel like this again, and as I came the second time, I started to cry.

"Are you okay?" he asked me. I nodded that I was, because I was too upset to speak, too certain I'd only cry harder if I did. I let him lay on top of me for a while, but when he moved, I went into comfort mode. I sat up, drawing my legs to my chest, and curling into a ball. I wanted to be as small as I could, to disappear, to pretend I wasn't responding like this. "I'm not okay," he confessed to me, saying what I couldn't say to him, telling me the things I was struggling with. Wrapping his arms around me, he said it again. "I'm definitely not okay."

I leaned into him and let him rub my back, let him play with my hair. "I'm sorry," I told him. "I really do want you to do this." I hiccupped, sputtering tears as I did.

"I know, babe," he said. "I know. I'm going to. But that doesn't mean it doesn't suck a whole hell of a lot right now. If I could go there and keep you, too, I would." I nodded. We were making the right choice.

Neither of us made the suggestion to try a relationship long-distance, to try to make it work when we were hours apart. The reality was this: I didn't want to hold him back. I didn't want to ask him to be with me when he went to another place. I wanted him to find something bigger and better than me, something that impacted him more. I wanted him to have the opportunity to forget me in ways I knew I'd never forget him. I wanted better for him than what I could ever be. So I let him hold me, and I let us share that moment of "what if?" and that moment of "I wish..." and then I let him fuck me one more time before the sun rose. That time, I didn't cry. I was out of tears.

At least, I thought I was out of tears until I got to the airport. His flight was boarding, and he had his arms around me, his face still buried in my neck. I knew he had to go. I knew that moment was goodbye. I kissed him and I let him kiss me. "I wish we had more time together," he told me. I agreed with him, I wished for it too. He pulled out a sheet of paper and handed it to me. "You better as hell not forget me, Connor Molina."

"I'm not going to forget you, Tris. You know that," I said.

I kissed him again. We said goodbye. And then he was gone.

Epilogue

Alex was rubbing me the wrong way. I didn't have time for his bullshit at all. I had to get to work, to be there and focus, to sit on stand and pay attention and instead he was getting me annoyed before I could get to work. The only benefit of this summer over the summer before, the summer I met Tristan, was that I didn't have to deal with school.

I could've gone home, sure, but there was something about being in the town I'd once called a hellhole. Springdale had grown on me the same way Tristan had. Hell, even Alex had grown on me, even if he was being annoying in the moment. But I'd gone from hating Springdale to feeling comfortable with it, and when I'd gone home for Christmas, things had felt wrong, like the place wasn't quite home. I missed where I'd been. So, for summer, I didn't make plans to go back. I applied at the pool, and I decided to stay. I don't know what possessed me to apply there. Maybe I liked torturing myself with old memories, bringing up a past I knew was long over in my mind. Tristan and I had tried to keep in touch. At first, we texted a lot, and that first month, we swapped more than a few dick pics.

Sometime around October, he'd gotten really invested in a project. I knew from social media and a few brief messages that he'd met someone too. I was happy for him, but when that ended, our conversations never really got back where they'd been before his relationship started. That was okay. I always wondered if he'd taken the time with him that he'd taken with me. I'd had a few hookups, too, but nothing like Tristan. Nothing that mattered to me.

It turned out the paper he gave me at the airport was a sketch, the one of our hands. It was probably stupid of me, but sometime around January I got it tattooed on my side, stretching from my waistline upwards. Just...our hands, interlocked. It wasn't like I'd gone and gotten his name on me. It was art, a sketch, and the outside world didn't have to know it reminded me of him every time I saw it in the mirror. One of the guys I hooked up with asked me about it. I said it was some art I found. I didn't go into details. How could I? It wasn't like I could say it was the love of my life's hand in mine, not when I wasn't supposed to consider Tristan the love of my life anyway. He was a summer fling and that was all.

A few times that year, I drove past Tristan's old house. Whoever bought it was doing a lot of work with it. They'd gutted it and flipped it, just like they'd promised they would, and the house looked nice. I wondered sometimes how Tristan would have felt knowing it wasn't the same house inside as it had been.

And yeah, through all of it, I still lived with Alex. He wasn't a half-bad roommate, not usually. The downside was the sublet. He had to go home that summer, and he was being a real prick about it.

"I don't know why you get to meet the guy and I don't," I snapped before work. "I'm the one who has to live with him."

"He's renting my room!" Alex yelled at me, tossing his clothes into his bag. "You're going to be at work before he can fly in. You really gonna call in sick on your first day of work to meet him? Chill, man. I'm just making sure he's not going to fuck up my place. You can sit there and get pissed all you want but do you really want to get stuck with the full rent payment this summer?"

I didn't. I just didn't understand what sort of asshole needed to fly in the day he was set to move in. That was stupid, and I was already certain I hated him. I hadn't even met him yet. In all the ways Tristan had taught me to be a better person, a nicer one, I was still annoyed now, still taking life more seriously than I should have. I knew it was a problem, and I couldn't figure out how to fix it.

The water at the pool got my mind off the sublet, both in a good way and a bad one. When Greg asked me to scrub toilets, I went into the supply room and closed the door. My mind, or at least the melancholy part that loved to torture itself, thought back to the times Tristan had surprised me in that very same room. I longed for him to come bounding in, for him to press me against the door, relive those old memories. But he didn't, and I was stuck scrubbing toilets and trying not to cry.

The year before had been easier than this, than being here and remembering all the reasons I'd fallen for him. All of it started with him being a goddamn idiot, and things were ending with me being just as hopeless and idiotic. I missed him. I wondered if anything in him missed me. I told myself I was probably being a little too ridiculous to think that.

After work, I drove home. My new roommate wasn't there yet, and I was annoyed all over again. Was I supposed to waste my day sitting around and waiting for him to come? Had he been there in the first place? I peeked in Alex's room, and clearly, he had. There was a nondescript suitcase just inside the door. I decided to lay down and nap.

I woke up when my bed shook with movement. I was startled awake and I wondered what sort of asshole walks into someone's room unannounced. What if I'd been naked or otherwise occupied? I tried to open my eyes. "Hey, pretty boy."

I think I almost died at the words. I sat up and wrapped my arms around him without even getting a good look at him. There was time for that later. Right now, I needed to feel him and make sure this wasn't some stupid dream, my brain playing tricks on my lonely heart. He ran his hand down my side. "I like this," he said, tracing my tattoo with his fingers. "I can't believe you got it on you forever."

"I promised I wouldn't forget you," I told him. "Kind of hard when your hand is on my body permanently." But then I felt self-conscious. "I'm sorry...is it weird? I should have asked..."

"It's not weird. I like it a lot," he promised. I leaned back and got a better look at him. He looked so good. He looked the same. He looked different. Mostly, he looked like I should have been dreaming but wasn't.

"Why are you here?" I asked him. I didn't mean for it to sound the way it did, but he chuckled.

"I thought it might be nice to come home for the summer," he said. "I thought it might be nice to come back to you. Are you mad?"

"No," I promised him. "I missed you," I said. I didn't care how cheesy it sounded. He needed to know.

"I missed you too," he told me. "I didn't think I could take a summer without you, Connor."

I kissed him, and just like always, he took things really slowly from there. I was thankful to have all summer to get to know him all over again.

He wasn't as wild this time, wasn't as reckless. We carpooled to work together, with me dropping him off at the construction firm he was a junior intern at a few blocks from the pool.

I didn't know what our lives would hold after summer. I didn't know if we'd make it or if his art school would break us again. But I had one more summer with Tristan and that's all I cared about. All I had to do was let go of my fear of this ending, and dive in.

Acknowledgements

Zachary, you save me every single day. Thanks for letting me do what I do, and for being such a blessing in my life. I don't know what I'd do without you. Maybe spend less on FIFA points, but I'd also be way less happy.

Ally, thanks for being the source of my sanity. Without the worlds you help me escape into, I'd never have made it this far. R+V forever.

Jeffrey, your work stories made this book what it is. I literally couldn't have written it without you and your gaggle of pool rats.

Jaime, Sky, Angelien, thank you for your feedback and help. This story is better because of you.

To The Bean team, thanks for letting me sit there for hours, and thanks for keeping me caffeinated while the pandemic wouldn't let me come in.

To everyone at NineStar Press who helped make this book a reality, I'm so thankful for your guidance, and to Elizabeth especially, I'm thankful for your patience with every extra instance of "that" you removed.

To the lifeguards who keep us safe all summer, thank you. And to those who didn't get to keep their summer job because of the state of the world this year, I hope next year is a better one for you.

And, for every Connor and Tristan who have yet to find each other, I hope you do. And I hope no one fakes a drowning in the process.

About the Author

J R Hart is a queer thirtysomething novelist passionate about telling romantic and erotic stories about LGBT+ characters. When J R isn't writing, you can find her at the science museum with her son, cheering for her favorite soccer team, or at The Bean Coffee Co plotting her next work. You can find her on Twitter and Instagram as @jrhartauthor, or on her website at jrhartauthor.com.

Email: jrhartauthor@gmail.com

Twitter: @jrhartauthor

Instagram: @jrhartauthor

Website: www.jrhartauthor.com

Other NineStar books by this author

This Christmas

Also Available from NineStar Press

Connect with NineStar Press

www.ninestarpress.com

www.facebook.com/ninestarpress

www.facebook.com/groups/NineStarNiche

www.twitter.com/ninestarpress